Buffalo Lake

-

A Charlie LeBeau Mystery

Gregory L. Heitmann

For the resilient.

A Charlie LeBeau Mystery

Many thanks to my family, gracias!

As always, a big thank you to my editors:

Angela

Dorene

Gwyneth

Front cover design by: Gregory L. Heitmann
Back cover photo credits: USDA and the author

Author's Note

This is a work of fiction and the usual rules apply. The characters, the conversations, and the incidents portrayed in this novel have been invented by the author. Nothing in this book is to be construed as real. Any resemblance to actual events, or persons, whether living or dead, is coincidental. Again, none of the characters are real. This is a fictional story conceived for entertainment purposes only.

Other novels by Gregory L. Heitmann:

Fort Sisseton – Dakota Territory

Chief Red Iron – The Lakota Uprising

The G MANN 2 – Pay-2-Play

Teener Baseball

Long Hollow – A Charlie LeBeau Mystery

Chapter 1

Lake Cabin

Day County, South Dakota

In the darkness, the soothing rhythm of waves lapping against the shore permeates the small cabin. The summer heat is mitigated by the breezes off the lake, and the windows and doors are wide open, screens in place to keep the mosquitoes at bay. The air circulates well. The cabin is a simple 850 square foot, two bedroom cottage. In addition to the bedrooms, a living room, kitchen, and bathroom make up the basic floor plan.

A lone figure dressed in black moves through darkness, illuminated only by the new moon and stars under the cloudless night sky. The late night visitor enters through the spring-loaded screen door in silence. The darkness of the cabin shrouds the figure as it moves to the back bedroom of the cabin where snores emanate.

The figure in black flicks the bedroom light on, and a sleeping gray-haired man awakens with a surprise. Squinting at the intruder, the decrepit man's eyes can not focus on the person in front of him. The old man finally reaches for his glasses on the bedside stand. He knocks over a black and white photo of his once younger self dressed in his black priest wardrobe, including his collar. The old, yellowed photo shows the young priest holding a small boy in front of a St. John's Catholic Church sign. Flanked on each side of the priest are three nuns and another priest.

The framed photo falls to the floor and shatters as the man, the now seventy-five year old retired priest, Father Michael Franzen gets his glasses in place. His head nods slowly. Still under the covers of his bed, he leans on an elbow, "Hmmph. It's you. My very own devil."

The figure in black, dressed like a modern-day ninja, points a gun at the priest, motioning him to get out of the bed. The old man refuses with a shake of his head and defiant smile. The intruder pulls the trigger, and a deafening roar cracks through the tiny bedroom. The bullet whizzes by the priest's ear, the headboard splinters, and the bullet lodges in the wall.

Father Franzen grunts, "Uhhhnn," as he grasps at his chest. He throws the bed sheet aside and moves unsteadily to his feet. The priest is shirtless, dressed only in boxers; his large round belly and chest are covered in silver hair. His thin legs seem incapable of supporting his rotund body. He holds his chest and gasps for air as he leans on the small dresser, the single piece of furniture in the bedroom besides the bed. "Help me," he pleads, his voice a husky rasp.

The intruder spies a gold cross buried in the gray chest hair of the priest. It hangs from a chain around the old man's neck. A black-gloved hand reaches out and tears the cross and chain from his neck. Father Franzen's body heaves. He pants, "I'm having a heart attack. If you are not going to help, just...just shoot me now."

The breathy words come as a whining plea. The aggressor, having no pity for the man, silently shakes its head, and motions the old man to walk. The stooped over priest manages to stagger toward the screen door of the cabin. Out the door the old man stumbles, bent almost in half, clutching at his chest. The visitor in black follows behind, the screen door on its spring restraint closes with a crack, like a small arms report.

Light spills from the cabin, providing harsh shadows on the shoreline. The assault continues on the old priest with a jab of the pistol into his ribs as they move toward the lake. From his stooped position, the priest eyes a canoe beached on the narrow strip of sandy shore. Crossing the short distance from the cabin to the stub of a dock protruding into the lake, the pair moves. The attacker prods the priest forward with pokes in the back from the barrel of the pistol. Stepping onto the dock, the old man stumbles, falling onto his belly. Rolling onto his back, the priest pleads with tears in his eyes, "For the love of Christ. I beg you..."

The attacker moves close to the incapacitated man, hovering over the wheezing priest, and extends the pistol, slowly, painstakingly aiming the weapon a few inches from the man's head. Prostrate on the dock, the man clutches at his chest with one hand, with the other he crosses himself and mumbles, "The Lord is my shepherd..."

He gasps for any hint of breath. He cannot finish the verse. With all his strength remaining, the priest speaks, "Father, please forgive them, they know not what they do."

The attacker's head shakes. Holding the weapon in one hand and with the other the cross and chain, the figure in black tosses the cross and chain in the lake. An almost imperceptible splash is heard as the items hit the water. In a grunting, guttural voice, the assaulter finally speaks, "You're wrong, Father. I know exactly what I do. Burn in hell, Father."

The assailant fires the weapon. The muzzle flash pierces the night, reflecting like a flash of lightning off the lake. The echo of the pistol's report roars one direction then the other in an eerie reverberation in the night air. The bullet splinters a wooden plank of the dock an inch from the priest's head. The old man's eyes widen and he gasps, choking a moment as he squeezes and clutches his chest. Then there is nothing but silence.

The assailant stands over the victim. A leg twitches as the attacker bends down, listening for a breath. Nothing. Mustering strength, the figure in black rolls the corpse off the dock into the water. With a gurgling splash the priest's body hits the water, forcing waves to wash along the shore from the disturbance on the still lake. The canoe grinds along the sandy beach, rocked by the waves.

The attacker looks around in the dark, surveying the surroundings while moving to the canoe. In a fluid motion the intruder pushes the canoe away from shore, gracefully leaping into the vessel, picking up the paddle, and silently stroking the water, skimming away from what appears to be a white-bellied whale, beached on the shore. The priest's body has returned to the earth, or to the water in this case, fish food.

Chapter 2

Fishermen

Buffalo Lake

On the southeast side of Buffalo Lake, just off Bureau of Indian Affairs Route 3, Charlie LeBeau relaxes on a Saturday morning fishing trip with his dad and his nephew. Waves lap at the shoreline of Buffalo Lake. Buffalo Lake is really a group of lakes that combine to form two bodies of water in wet years, or in dry years, several individual lakes. Located eleven miles west of Sisseton, South Dakota, Buffalo Lake forms its own district and community on the Sisseton-Wahpeton Indian Reservation. The reservation covers the heart of the Coteau Des Prairies, "the slope on the prairie." The Coteau was carved and shaped by the glaciers ten thousand years ago. The lands feature the Glacial Lakes Region in the higher elevations, areas gouged by the glaciers, but not scarred smooth by the ancient seas that flattened the plains. The hills of the Glacial Lakes Region are dotted with hundreds, if not thousands, of bodies of water. The Coteau juts up steeply in the flat land on its east and west sides, rising 350 feet in a mile or so. Along the South Dakota Highway 10 corridor, the Coteau begins in earnest about three miles west of Sisseton and continues for approximately twenty-five miles through rolling terrain before dropping into the remnants of the leveled fertile grounds of the James River Valley and the town of Britton.

The Sisseton-Wahpeton Indian Reservation is predominantly defined by the Coteau on its eastern and western boundaries. The reservation's north and south limits also relate to the Coteau. Starting at a point just north of what is now Watertown, South Dakota, it was said that an Indian chief held his arms in a "V" as he faced to the north and declared his tribal bands' lands with the north boundary barely jutting into what is now the southern border of North Dakota. The lands of these Lakota people, the Santee bands of the Sisseton and the Wahpeton people, were reduced to approximately 165 square miles in the 1860s.

The modern day reservation is home to a sportsman's paradise of hunting, fishing, and boating, as well as the dominant agricultural economy of the Dakotas. Many of the Glacial Lakes sport a thriving community of vacation cabins. The bigger, deeper lakes like Roy, Clear, and Pickerel, have a mix of seasonal cabin dwellers and permanent residents. Buffalo Lake, a shallower lake, has limited accessible shore line and is an off-the-beaten-path sort of getaway.

The men enjoy a peaceful morning of solitude under near perfect June skies and weather. The base of operations is just off the highway fifty yards or so. Charlie's truck is parked at the end of the two rut trail that provides access to the shore. The trail ends, blocked by a tangle of scrub oak, ash, and mature oak trees, but it is the ideal entry point to today's fishing spot. Dropping down from the truck, descending a two-foot cut bank formed by the wave action of an exceptionally high water mark, the fishermen have staked their claim with lawn chairs, tackle boxes, and bait buckets.

Charlie LeBeau, Bureau of Indian Affairs police Sergeant, has the weekend off to enjoy with family. Charlie is approaching his mid-forties now with fifteen years on the force. He looks ten years younger than his birth age, the product of good genetics and conservative living. An enrolled member of the Sisseton-Wahpeton Sioux Tribe, Charlie returned to the reservation having seen his satisfactory share of the world with a stint in the Army, including a tour in Desert Storm. He is a good looking man. His Native American features comingle with his surname's lineage; he is a hybrid. His French-European ancestry combines perfectly with his Lakota blood. A symmetrical face is punctuated by piercing blue eyes.

Charlie's father, Claude, sits in the early morning sun on his lawn chair, watching his bobber on the lake, fighting reflected sunrays off the choppy water. "I thought you said they were bitin'?" Claude states with just a hint of whininess.

Claude LeBeau is seventy-three years old. He is a snapshot of Charlie thirty years from now. His thick hair is white, quite a stark contrast to his deeply tanned skin. To look at him, you would never guess he was an enrolled member of the Sisseton-Wahpeton Sioux Tribe. The dominant physical characteristics of his ancient relatives from the Gaul region in Western Europe disguise his Native American bloodlines. One might guess Claude is in his 60s, since he stays fit and, for the most part, active for his age.

Charlie's only response to his father's complaint is a shrug of his shoulders as he sits a few yards from his father, resting his behind on the cut bank, staring at his own red and white bobber bouncing on the waves of the lake. He sheds his Minnesota Twins baseball cap for a moment to run his fingers through his hair, now sporting a bristling gray hair here and there in the shock of black locks.

Claude yells over his shoulder, toward his grandson, Nathaniel Chasing Hawk, "Any luck?"

Nat Chasing Hawk, nephew of Charlie, grandson of Claude, has been an orphan for almost a year. His father, best friends with Charlie, died just out of the police academy, hit by a drunk driver while on patrol. Nat never met his father. Tragedy hit again for Nat five years ago when his mother was diagnosed with breast cancer. She fought a long, hard fight, succumbing last fall, leaving Charlie in charge of raising her son through his final teenage years. Claude and Charlie had always been an integral part in Nat's upbringing, before taking on the full time task.

It is no surprise that Nat is the stellar athlete in the community. Following in the footsteps of his uncle and mentor, Nat has been a star basketball player since he was a freshman in high school. As an all-state basketball honorable mention, even with an injury his junior year, the college recruiters have salivated over this six foot three, wiry shooting guard. Charlie has succumbed to his young protégé on the driveway basketball court lately, due to the effect of age giving way to youth as bodies mature and break down. But it's another game today. Today Nat tries to translate his skill with a rod and reel to dominate the waters. Everything is a competition among these three generations of men. Today the questions include: "Who will catch the biggest fish?" and "Who will catch the most fish?"

Nat casts his Rapala, imitation-minnow lure, twenty yards into the lake as he stands on shore. He reels slowly and steadily, jerking the tip of the rod every few seconds. "You hear me?" Claude shouts again, "Any luck?"

"Shhh, you'll scare the fish," Charlie tries to shush his father.

Nat shakes his head in disgust. "Nada," he shouts back.

Nat is much darker skinned than his uncle and grandfather. His dad was an enrolled member of the Oglala Sioux Tribe from the Pine Ridge Indian Reservation. It was Charlie that introduced his sister to Nat's dad. Roommates at the BIA police academy, the men became fast friends, and soon after, family. Charlie is a default father to Nat, the young man standing on shore in his everyday uniform of blue jeans and white t-shirt. As Charlie looks at his nephew concentrating on casting and reeling, he appreciates his life today in a manner he never thought imaginable.

Claude shifts in the flimsy lawn chair, head shaking. "Slow day. Where'd you get your fishing report?"

Charlie throws up his hands in a shrug of defensiveness, "Skip told me that he overheard Jerry Decker sayin' Buffalo Lake was hot."

Claude points a bony finger at his son, "Well, let him know he dropped the ball on this one."

Charlie waves away the accusing finger, "Bah, just relax. It's a nice day."

"Yeah," Claude nods, "but it could be a beautiful day with a lakeside fish fry."

"Dad, can you do me a favor?" Charlie smiles. "Could you at least not complain the rest of morning?"

Claude laughs, "I'm just sayin,' there are fifty lakes within a half hour of our house, and we manage to find one with no fish in it."

"Dad, I'll make you a deal. Next time, you find out where they're biting."

Father and son quickly have their attention diverted to the shore. "Whoa!" Nat calls out.

The drag on Nat's fishing reel squeals. "I got one!" Nat yells. Nat reels furiously, and the drag sizzles wildly as it eases the pressure on the line. The rod is bent in a perfect "J" shape. "It feels like a good one!"

Charlie and Claude stand simultaneously and move close to Nat.

"Easy. Careful now," Claude cautions.

"You need the net?" Charlie asks.

"Oh," Nat's shoulders slump, and he slows his retrieve. "Never mind. It's just a log or something." Nat continues to reel, walking backwards a bit as he drags the object closer.

"Hey!" Claude shouts and points, "Looks like a cooler."

The fish-shaped lure with three sets of treble hooks has embedded a barb into the woven nylon-strap of a small, soft-sided, insulated lunch cooler, about the size of a breadbox. Charlie reaches down and picks up the soggy container. It is sealed on top by a zipper cover. "It's got somebody's name on it," Charlie remarks with a surprise. Charlie reads the name written in Sharpie pen on the top, "Susan Montgomery."

Charlie unhooks the lure from the strap. Claude points to Charlie smiling and providing a running commentary, "At least we didn't get skunked! Open it! See if we got ourselves some lunch in lieu of a fish fry. Unzip it!"

With a nod, Charlie proceeds to unzip the cover and drain water from the saturated, small, cubicle cooler. After most of the water is removed, he fully unzips the container for a full inspection. "Let's see, we got a sandwich in a bag, looks like it's still dry, a coke, a pickle…" Charlie pushes to the bottom of the cooler. "What else we got in here?" Charlie stops digging. He peers down to the bottom of the cooler, staring stock-still for a moment. He glances up, looking at Nat and Claude. "A box of .45 caliber shells?" Charlie turns his observational statement into a question.

Claude laughs, "Susan Montgomery and a box of bullets? Now that's funny."

Nat looks at Charlie with a puzzled look on his face, "Who's Susan Montgomery?"

Charlie shakes his head, "You know her. She's Veronica's new employee at the paper."

"Oh, yeah! That older lady," Nat nods. "Why would she have a box of shells in her lunchbox?"

Claude laughs some more, "The shells aren't the most unusual thing, are they, Charlie?" Charlie smiles. "Ms. Montgomery," Claude continues, "was Charlie's fourth grade teacher, and she used to be a nun. Isn't that right, Charlie?"

Nat laughs and looks at his uncle with questioning eyes.

Charlie shrugs and laughs. "I'll see that she gets her cooler back."

Claude holds up a finger, "Make sure you ask her about her .45s."

Charlie nods, "I definitely will."

The excitement of Nat's snag has ebbed, and Charlie looks around the lake. "What do you think? Should we call it a day?" He looks back and forth between his father and nephew, waiting for confirmation.

"Give me ten more casts," Nat states.

Charlie twists his mouth with a nod, "All right."

Nat steps to the edge of shore and lets loose with a long cast next to the edge of this year's growth of cattails. "I wish Mom was still here. She was always the luckiest fisherman."

Charlie and Claude smile at instant memories of fishing with Corrine, Nat's mother. "Yeah, she sure was," Charlie affirms Nat's statement.

Charlie is amazed that Nat seems comfortable in recalling his mother's life. For Charlie, he still is susceptible to choke up when thinking of his sister, still less than a year ago since she died. Charlie watches Nat cast again and reel the lure quickly, jerking the rod intermittently. As Charlie stares at the water, his mind is taken back to the news of Corrine announcing her cancer diagnosis to the family: that devastating supper time announcement when everything changed. It was a repeat of their own mother, diagnosed at a much later age, but battling breast cancer in her sixties. Corrine fought bravely like her mother, never a discouraging word of defeat; still the disease claimed her five years later at the age of thirty-seven. Charlie shakes that image from his mental picture, replacing it with his sister's smiling face, standing right where Nat stands this morning. The memory of Corrine reeling in jumbo-sized perch cast after cast will never be erased from Charlie's memory.

Nat casts again. The lure plunking down simultaneously with the buzz of Charlie's phone in his shirt pocket. The seemingly synchronized combination of phone call and lure splash down, illicit an "Uh-oh," from Nat. "You gettin' called in?"

Charlie retrieves the phone from his pocket and checks the incoming call on the phone's screen. "Maybe. It's Skip." Charlie presses the "answer" button on the phone, "Hello."

Charlie listens as he watches Nat continue to cast. "Yeah, Buffalo Lake. By the way, thanks for nothing on your fishing report. Not a bite."

Charlie smiles as he listens to his boss on the other end of the line. He nods, "Sure. I can see his cabin directly across from us. We're headin' out right now. Nat's got about five more casts to change our luck."

Charlie listens a moment before finishing the call, "I'll let you know."

Charlie pushes the "end call" button on his phone and stows the phone back in his shirt pocket. "Skip's got trouble?" Claude questions.

Charlie purses his lips and shakes his head, "Just a welfare check on the old priest, Father Franzen. He was supposed to pick up some medication at the pharmacy a few days ago. Nobody's seen him and no answer on his phone. We'll go check it out."

Chapter 3

Scavengers

The fishing rods and gear are stowed in the bed of Charlie's pickup truck, and the men climb into the cab of the late 1980's Ford. Nat scoots his way to the center of the cloth bench seat, "Geez, Uncle Charlie, when you gonna get a new truck? Can't you get a four-door? I'm sick of being stuck in the middle all the time."

Claude chimes in with a grin plastered on his face, "Yeah, Charlie. When ya gettin' a new truck?"

Charlie rolls his eyes and shakes his head as he eases behind the wheel. "I work for the government. This is what I can afford." Charlie forces a smile, "And it gets the job done just fine."

Charlie turns the key in the ignition, and the truck's engine fires up with a rumble. Charlie reaches out and pats the dashboard. "Good girl. Don't listen to them. You're a good truck."

"I must admit," Nat nods. "It does sound awesome. It's got that big gas guzzlin' V-8 engine."

Charlie puts the truck in reverse and backs down the trail toward the highway. He gets the vehicle turned around and onto the paved BIA highway, heading north a mile and a half following the curving shore of the lake. Climbing up a small slope a few feet, exiting the historic basin of the lake, Charlie finds his turn and hangs a left on the gravel section-line road. The trio proceeds in silence. They head west on the county maintained road, gravel kicking up on the underside of the truck as Charlie proceeds at a casual speed. The AM radio station softly plays the Beatles' "You've Got To Hide Your Love Away." John Lennon's tinny, straining vocals are barely audible over the road noise. Claude finally breaks the silence, "So, what's the deal with our nun and her cooler, Sister Susan. She's in town for a while?"

Charlie looks over at his father a moment before turning his eyes back to the road. "I'm pretty sure you know all about her, Dad."

Claude smiles wryly.

"How long has she been back, a year?" Charlie answers his own question. "I know she's been working with Veronica, helping at the paper for almost nine months."

Claude raises his eyebrows, "Huh, news to me. Get it...news...newspaper?" Claude laughs at his own joke, elbowing Nat.

"Good one, Grandpa," Nat mumbles stoically as he bounces along in the middle of the seat.

"Nothing like a newspaper joke," Claude chortles still.

The straight mile-section road swings around the north edge of Buffalo Lake before intersecting another mile-section road. The mile-square section-line roads that form grids across the Great Plains farmland, the product of the Homestead Act, lose some of their integrity due to all the lakes and ponds in the Glacial Lakes Region. Charlie turns left on the gravel road, pointing the vehicle south, the final leg on the circuitous route around the lake. Ahead a mile or so, Charlie can see the trees ringing the west shore of the lake where the cabin is located.

They approach the driveway to the priest's cabin; Charlie is now in police officer mode and noting to himself the section road continuing to the west. On the north side of the road another cattail-lined slough abuts the road. Further to the west, the section road appears to end at a tree-encircled farmstead. Charlie scrunches his face as he tries to remember the family that lives there. He can make out the edge of the barn mostly shrouded by, large, impressive blue spruce evergreen trees probably planted forty years ago and providing a perfect windbreak. The name finally registers in Charlie's head, "Hostettler's," Charlie says aloud.

"Huh?" Claude looks at Charlie.

"I was just trying to remember the family over there," Charlie pushes his chin toward the farmstead.

"Yeah, that's Hostettler's," Claude confirms.

Charlie slows to make the turn to the south, from the section road to the cabin's driveway. He stops.

"Uh-oh," Charlie murmurs. "I don't like the looks of this." Charlie points at a flock of crows swooping down from their high position in a tall cottonwood tree's exposed dead branches. The flock disappears behind the smaller trees surrounding the lake, but several crows appear, rising to replace their departing feathered friends roosting in the dead branches of the cottonwood,.

"Crows," Charlie says quietly. He points again over the lake. "I see some sea gulls circling."

"What do you mean?" Nat questions.

"Scavengers," Claude nods in confirmation.

"Something's probably dead," Charlie frowns.

"The old priest?" Claude's question is almost a statement.

Charlie's mouth twists. "You guys stay with the truck when we get up there."

"I can take it," Nat counters.

Charlie looks to his nephew as he eases the vehicle forward, parking next to the priest's old, faded-red Nissan Sentra. Killing the engine of his truck and pulling on the door handle, he eyes Nat a moment before turning his attention to Claude. "And you, Dad?"

"I'm fine," Claude shrugs, pulling on his door handle. "We'll check it out together."

"It could be bad," Charlie warns as he exits the truck along with his father and nephew.

"Let's just go," Claude waves a hand and pushes forward.

"Hold up," Charlie speaks sharply. He draws a snub-nosed .38 caliber revolver from his ankle holster. "You guys stay behind me."

Chapter 4

Discovery

Charlie leads the group forward. The men look through the windows of the priest's car. Charlie tries the door, and it opens. The keys are in the ignition, and a buzz sounds a warning of the door ajar. Charlie notices the neatly kept interior of the vehicle and the smell of pine as he spies the air freshener hanging from the rearview mirror. Charlie eases the door to a closed position, latching it quietly. He holds a finger to his lips as an indicator to Claude and Nat to keep silent. He waves his hand to his followers as he begins to move forward, toward the cabin. Charlie points behind him where he wants them to walk, following closely, but not too closely.

The group covers the twenty yards to the cabin slowly and steadily. The "caw" of a crow echoes from the lakeside. Charlie places a hand on the cabin's rough siding. He looks behind, extends a finger, and without a word, communicates to his companions to stay, as if commanding a dog. Charlie moves forward, alone, into the lakeside yard. He extends his arms holding his .38 at the ready. The large oak trees shade the grass and narrow beach. The din of crows and seagulls goes silent. As Charlie pushes down the slope toward the water, a dozen crows take flight in a rush of wings, scattering into the slightest of breezes. Their flight spooks several sea gulls. Charlie whispers to himself, "Too many birds to be a good sign."

The crows' departure reveals Charlie's suspicions. He lowers his weapon and moves forward to the bloated white corpse of Father Franzen, bobbing on the shore. Charlie waves Nat and Claude forward as he bends down and stows his pistol in his ankle holster. As he stands he draws his cell phone and moves forward to within a few feet of the body.

Claude and Nat move down to the shore, stopping a couple yards away, "Oh, boy," Claude groans, looking from the body to Charlie.

Charlie pushes the send button and places the phone to his ear, "Hey, Skip. Bad news. Call the coroner. We got a floater."

Charlie listens a moment. He looks back to his nephew and father, shaking his head. "Yeah, it's Franzen. He's a mess. Bloated. Scavengers have gotten to him."

Charlie listens some more. He nods, "I'll wait, but I got my dad and nephew with me."

Charlie nods again, making eye contact with his father. Claude waves away Charlie's look. "Don't worry about us," Claude frowns.

"Ok, I'll send them home," Charlie states as he ends the call.

Charlie waves at his dad and nephew, "Come on down! You want to come down and take a look?"

Claude and Nat move cautiously, covering the few yards between them and the body ever so slowly. They follow Charlie up on the dock and look down at the body, rocking gently in the waves. "What do you think happened, Charlie?" Claude questions with an exaggerated frown.

Charlie shrugs, "He was an old man. Skip told me he was on heart medicine and hadn't picked it up at the pharmacy. That's why we came here to do a welfare check on him." Charlie's shoulders go up and down again, "Guess old age probably got him."

Claude points at the corpse, "Out here in his boxers?"

Charlie's head shakes, and he shrugs again.

Nat points to the body, "Wow. The birds were really starting to do a number on him."

Charlie nods, "Yeah, I've seen much worse. I'd guess he's been out here a couple days already."

"What are we gonna do?" Nat looks inquisitively at his uncle.

"We are not going to do anything," Charlie smiles. "I'm waiting here. You guys take the truck home. It's probably going to be a long day. Skip will give me a ride home when we're done."

Charlie tosses the keys to Nat. "I'll walk you up."

The trio moves up the slope, past the cabin, and back to the driveway. "Don't wait up, I might be awhile. Sorry 'bout the fishin'. We'll have to try again." Charlie gives a nod to his dad. "When Claude gets a good scouting report."

Claude returns the smile from his son, "Don't you worry. I'll find the next hotspot soon enough."

Chapter 5

A Whale of a Case

Charlie gives a final wave to Nat and Claude as they back down the driveway and onto the gravel road in his old truck. He's alone. Turning back to face the lake he notices the tall prairie grass starting to bend in the breeze. From the priest's cabin to the county road, the lot is covered in tall, un-mowed grass. A strip of Kentucky blue grass about ten yards wide lines the lakeside frontage of the cabin. The landscape opposite the lake and adjacent to the driveway is that of an un-mowed hayfield. As Charlie makes his way back to the lakeside of the cabin, he notices the ancient gas-powered lawn mower resting against the cabin. Charlie smiles as he sees the insignia of the now long defunct Coast-to-Coast hardware store symbol still encrusted on the deck of the mower.

Charlie moves from the sunshine to the covered porch on the shore-side of the cabin. He moves to the edge of the porch and picks up a small stick, discarded by the towering oak above. The Kentucky blue grass on the lake side of the cabin is thin and patchy, stunted by the shade from the trees. The tiny porch sports two chairs, a rocking chair, and an old-fashioned, clam-shell-backed metal chair, rusted with age.

Turning his attention to the cabin's single entrance, Charlie notes the inside, solid door is open, but the screen door is closed. He uses the stick to hook the simple handle of the screen door on just the outside chance that there might be finger prints to retrieve. Straining the spring held door against his stick, the thin branch breaks, and the door slams with a crack. Charlie flinches at the snapping branch and slamming door. He smiles to himself as he retrieves another tool, a more stout stick to leverage the door open.

Inside the cabin Charlie observes the compact living quarters. "Nothing out of the ordinary," he murmurs to himself.

Everything seems to be in its place as he moves from the small kitchen combined living room area to a bedroom. The clock-radio on the nightstand comes to life, rattling its tiny speaker with a tune from Seals & Kroft, "Diamond Girl." A startled Charlie instinctively grabs at his hip for his weapon, then quickly his ankle holster when he realizes he doesn't have his uniform on. He laughs to himself at his reaction, realizing the threat is a late morning alarm setting. He moves to the nightstand and clicks off the alarm, careful to not disturb any potential prints.

Charlie's eyes immediately lock onto the splintered headboard. The light-colored scarred wood is like a beacon to his eye. He moves from the doorway to the wooden headboard, noting the unmade bed, blanket and sheet flung to the side, as if someone had exited in a hurry. Charlie grasps his chin in thought as he inspects the downward trajectory of the likely bullet hole. Careful not to disturb anything, he scans for any trace of blood. There is none. The broken picture frame holding the photo of the priest lies scattered on the floor next to the bed. He stands in the room, staring at the bed. Minutes pass as his mind plays out what might have happened. He ponders the situation, imagined events rolling through his mind. The "caw" of a crow finally snaps him back to his surroundings, and he moves back to the living room, through the door, and back out onto the porch.

The bravest or hungriest crow has returned to the bobbing body in the water, but Charlie's appearance on the porch frightens the bird back to a tree fifty yards away where it rejoins its flock to a raucous greeting. Charlie turns his attention back to the blob in the water. The corpse reminds him of a miniature, beached whale, the kind you sometimes hear about on the news.

He looks to the left. The nearest cabin is about three hundred yards away. To his right is the Hostettler farmstead about a half mile away. Their farmstead is the end of the line on the country road. Buffalo Lake on its south side and a series of small sloughs guard its flanks, the only approach is from the east by the gravel road. This cabin, and the surrounding neighbors, are very secluded, isolated even by the standards of rural South Dakota.

Charlie moseys off the porch and down the narrow concrete sidewalk with intermittent steps down in elevation to the narrow beach and onto the stubby dock. He hadn't noticed it initially, but there it was, plain as day now in the sun light. The splintered hole in the wooden plank of the dock is very conspicuous now. The sun has moved in the sky now, and its beams avoid the oak trees and shine down on the weathered boards of the dock. Again, there is no sign of blood in the surrounding area.

Charlie moves to the end of the dock and enjoys the cool breeze on his face. The wind is picking up and blows refreshingly across the water. The waves roll into shore, a little bigger now. The rhythmic sloshing of water is hypnotic, and Charlie closes his eyes for a moment as the warmth of the sun and the cool lake breeze battle for dominance on his skyward-pointed face. It would be a perfect summer day, if not for the body lolling in the water next to the dock.

Charlie shakes his head. He looks at his watch, "Dang it," he says quietly, "Should have had those guys leave me a sandwich."

Charlie moves off the dock, trudging up the narrow, hand-poured, concrete sidewalk, he moves slowly, making his way back to the porch. He notes a rocking chair. He resists the temptation to sit and feel the worn-smooth handles. He looks across the lake and spies a lone boat on the lake. Two occupants appear to be holding fishing rods as the boat moves slowly into the wind, trolling for fish.

Chapter 6

Skip

The breeze rustling through the leaves is enough to mask the approach of Bureau of Indian Affairs Police Captain Skyler "Skip" Kipp's Police Tahoe. The slamming of the Tahoe door gets Charlie's attention, and he peers around the corner of the cabin before stepping fully around the building and walking to greet his boss. Skip is in uniform as he nonchalantly moves toward the cabin. Charlie raises a hand in greeting and welcomes the police commander, "What took you so long? Did you have to clean and press your uni?"

Skip rolls his eyes as the men approach each other for a handshake. "Yeah," Skip waves a hand at the Tahoe, "also hand-washed the truck."

Skip grins. "How's your weekend goin'?"

Charlie shakes his head as the men turn toward the lake and begin walking. "Just peachy."

Skip's smile widens, exaggerating his chipmunk-like features, slightly buck teeth and high cheek bones, the kind little rodents stuff full of seeds. Captain Kipp is forty-eight years old and eligible to retire, but he loves his job. He's the sort of man that's been frozen in the time period of the 80s. His mullet hair cut is parted down the middle when not in short braids. Skip's a half a foot shorter than Charlie's six foot stature, but his commanding presence is still powerful. He is a respected leader in law enforcement, in the community, and in his tribe.

The men amble slowly toward the shore. "What's the rush?" Skip questions, still with a grin. "He's still dead, isn't he?"

Charlie gives a little laugh, and for the first time, Skip can look down the slope and see the white blob on the shore. Skip stops walking. "Yup, I see 'im. He's definitely dead."

Charlie laughs again at the gallows humor. It's always uncomfortable dealing with the dead, but the police brotherhood has coping mechanisms, such as the morbid humor. Skip looks to Charlie with a grin, "What were you sayin' about the rush?"

Charlie just shakes his head as the men begin descending the narrow concrete path down to the dock. "I was saying," Charlie speaks low and slow, "there is no rush. I already got this case half-solved."

"Half-solved, eh?" Skip questions. "I need whole-solved, but tell me what ya got, Sherlock?"

"Somebody wanted this old man to hurry up and die," Charlie explains matter-of-factly.

Skip's eyes widen as the pair shuffles down the slope, "Oh, really?" Skip points to the body as they reach the sandy shoreline, "Yup, he's definitely dead."

The policemen step onto the dock, "Thank you, Dr. Skip," Charlie quips. "What was your first clue?"

Skip purses his lips, "First clue was the smell."

Charlie laughs, "Where'd you get that medical degree of yours again? Alco?"

Skip shrugs the comment off with a smile, "So, you were sayin' we got a murder? He just didn't forget his pills and keel over?"

Charlie shakes his head, "That's highly unlikely." He points a finger at his feet, "It's a weird one." Charlie squats down and points at the bullet hole in the dock. "It's fresh. Somebody put a bullet in...well, through really, the dock. No blood." Charlie gives a nod toward the cabin as he stands. "Same as in the headboard in the bedroom."

Skip squats down and touches the splintered orifice left by the slug. "Humph," Skip rises to his full height, "Look at his body. He's got all kinds of wounds."

The bloated, white corpse rises and falls with each sloshing wave. Gashes, nicks, and tears of all shapes and sizes scar the pale flesh. Charlie shakes his head in refute of the comment, "Those are from the gulls and crows. We chased whole flocks of birds off him. What do you think? Dead a couple days?"

Skip purses his lips and cocks his head as he stares at the body, "At least."

The men stare in silence from their position on the dock. Each man is lost in his own thoughts, imagining the brutal death of the man floating before them. Skip breaks his gaze from the body and looks at Charlie. "So, you got this half-solved? What's your theory? Somebody fired a gun at close range, hoping to give the guy a heart attack?"

"That's about the gist of it, I reckon," Charlie drawls. "And, it looks like they succeeded. Won't know for sure until the medical examiner gives us a report."

Skip can't stop shaking his head as he turns his eyes back to the dead man. "It's too bad we couldn'ta waited a few more days. The scavengers woulda processed him, and we would have a missing person's report. A one pager, instead we're gonna have ten days of non-stop paperwork."

Charlie can't help but laugh, "So cynical, it's all about you, isn't it?"

Skip's shoulders dip, "Kinda. Yeah, pretty much."

"No," Charlie begins. "It's good for the family to have closure. It'd be terrible on the family to never know what happened. This way they can have their funeral."

"Yeah," Skip nods. "You're right. There's just one thing about your theory...who would want to kill an old priest? What in heaven's name would be the motive?"

Skip laughs heartily. "Get it?" Skip continues to snicker. "Heaven's name? Cuz he's a priest."

Charlie shakes his head slowly and smiles. "Yeah, hilarious, George Carlin. You are right though; it beats me on the motive question."

Charlie looks toward the cabin and the road. "When's the cavalry comin'? I thought we'd have first responders and the whole she-bang out here."

"Clyde was preparing for a funeral. Mrs. Williams, remember her?"

Charlie's brow furrows. "She was in the rest home. Wasn't she like a hundred and three?"

"Yup. She passed away. I told him no rush," Skip removes his hat, pushes his hair back, and resets his policeman's cap. "We probably got a couple hours before the recovery team gets here."

Charlie steps off the dock, moving up the slope, "Come on. I'll show you the bullet hole in the bedroom."

Skip follows Charlie, "All right."

"Did you call the FBI?" Charlie throws out the question.

"What do you think?" Skip responds defensively as they climb the slope.

"I'd say that a murder on the reservation is gonna bring them running."

"Ha," Skip retorts. "I didn't know it was a murder when I called them. Just a dead priest. Nonetheless, Agent Brown is on his way."

"I knew it!" Charlie calls out.

The men step up on the cabin's porch and look back at the body and then out to the lake. Skip shakes his head, "Sure'd be a nice view, if it wasn't for that body floatin' right there."

"You can say that again," Charlie chimes in.

The cool lake breeze rustles the leaves. "Come on," Charlie motions. "See if you can find the bullet hole."

Charlie pries open the screen door with his stick he had used before. Skip follows Charlie inside. "Hey," Skip says demurely, "about my jokes and the priest; don't tell my wife I said that."

"Don't worry, Boss," Charlie laughs, "Those words are safe with me. You can go to confession for your sacrilege."

Chapter 7

Fragile

Charlie's manufactured home sits just a few miles west of Sisseton. On a two acre plot granted to him by the tribal council ten years ago, Charlie set up his homestead in a place he had loved since his boyhood. His home rests in the heart of his favorite whitetail deer hunting territory. His tribal allotment was part of a forty acre tribal trust parcel surrounded by private holdings. Adjacent to the tree-lined coulee that drains the Coteau Des Prairies to the west, his home shares residence with the cornfields of his friendly neighbors that have granted Charlie exclusive rights to pursue one of his favorite pastimes, deer hunting.

This time of year the corn in the fields is tall and green. The towering oak trees standing guard along the drainages are lush with their own green, distinctly shaped leaves. A wet spring and summer is producing projected bumper crops. The setting is a beautiful, constant reminder of man's relationship with nature. For Charlie, he thinks of his blessed life in rural South Dakota as just a lucky turn of fate. He has everything he would want or need right where he is. He feels sorry for those people trapped in town. Charlie's father routinely chides him saying, "Geez, Charlie, you only have three seasons in your year, hunting season, last hunting season, or next hunting season."

Charlie always laughs and responds with the same reply, "That's not true, Dad. You always forget football season."

Tuesday night is chicken night at the LeBeau household. Charlie stopped at the Super Valu and picked up the two rotisserie chickens as per the usual routine. As Charlie exits his BIA Police Tahoe, he sees his resident flock of wild turkeys disappear into the wooded coulee. He watches the heads of the parent turkeys bob through the grass, rounding up their chicks hidden by the prairie foliage. Charlie looks to his plastic sack of supermarket prepared chicken and back to the wild turkeys blending into their habitat. In a blink of an eye they are gone, camouflaged by the scrub oaks along the banks of the trickling stream. "If only," Charlie looks again at the plastic bags in his hands and then to the spot where the turkeys disappeared. He shakes his head and bounces up the steps to his front door.

Inside his house, Charlie is welcomed home. "Hey, Charlie," Claude calls out from his favorite La-Z-Boy chair, as he lounges with the TV remote in hand flipping channels.

From the kitchen Nat gives a wave to Charlie, "Biscuits are done. Just finishing the mac and cheese."

Charlie holds up the bag of chicken, "I'm done cookin'."

He moves to the dining room table. His humble home boasts a combined kitchen, dining room, and living room. The kitchen divides the master suite on one side and the two bedrooms on the other. Setting the chicken on the table, Charlie turns to his dad, "Let's eat."

Claude pushes on the handle of the recliner's leg rest mechanism, lowers it, and eases himself from the chair. "Uf-dah," Claude stands with a groan. "How was your day, Charlie?"

Charlie shrugs as he removes the chicken from the bags and stows the plastic grocery bags in a larger bag inside a low cabinet under the counter. "Still working on the priest."

Nat brings the biscuits and macaroni to the table. "Ready?"

The men sit and Charlie reaches for a biscuit, but before he can grab one, his father stops him. "Speaking of priests, should we give some thanks?"

Charlie and Nat look at each other and then to Claude, finally back to each other. This isn't a common occurrence. Maybe, Thanksgiving and Easter, there might be a prayer, but a routine, evening meal? This was not typical.

"Go ahead," Charlie shrugs.

"Thank you, Father," Claude closes his eyes, "for these gifts." Claude pauses a moment before continuing, "The food and family. Amen." Claude opens his eyes and smiles at his supper table companions.

"Amen," Charlie and Nat chime in.

"Let's eat," Nat grabs the mac and cheese and scoops a heaping spoonful onto his plate.

The men sit in silence eating and enjoying the meal. Charlie finally interrupts the peace and quiet. "I saw the turkeys headin' for the coulee when I got home."

Both Nat and Claude nod in acknowledgment as they chew on their respective pieces of chicken. The group is in silence again. It's Nat that breaks the silence as he tears a drumstick from the chicken and sets it on his plate. He licks his fingers as he eyes his uncle. "Do you ever get used to it, Uncle Charlie?"

"Used to what?" Charlie responds, puzzled by the question.

"Death," Nat says quietly.

"No," Charlie shakes his head. "I don't."

Nat takes a bite of his drumstick. He wipes his mouth with a napkin as he looks at his uncle. "That's the only body I've ever seen, besides my mom."

Charlie pulls at the chunk of the golden-brown, crusted-skin covering his chicken breast on his plate. "Life is very fragile. A lot of people forget that." Charlie holds a piece of his chicken on a fork. "Probably ninety five percent of people have no grasp that the chicken they eat was a living breathing creature. They don't make a connection to life and other living things."

It is quiet again. Claude looks back and forth between the youth on each side of the table before him. "You can't be scared of death, or life for that matter. I look around the reservation, and I see plenty people alive but not living. A lot of our Indian brothers and sisters seem to be more scared of living life than death. There's a balance. You can't be scared of death; you got to respect it. Appreciate it. But don't be scared of it."

Nat reaches for another biscuit and tears it open. "Death always makes me think of my mom."

Claude's head bobs, "We all miss her. It's all that much more important for you to live your life, not just exist. To honor her memory."

Nat washes down a mouthful with a drink of milk. "It was definitely a wakeup call the other day, seeing that dead body."

Charlie chews and swallows. "It's good to be reminded. I think about it almost every day when I just look outside. This is deer country, and I think about deer hunting every day. That makes me think about life and death; that puts food on the table for us." Charlie winces and holds up a piece of white breast meat from his piece of chicken. "Well, not tonight with this corporate-chicken-farm product, but you know what I mean."

"Changing the subject a bit," Claude interjects, "back to real life. How's the baseball going? When's the next game?"

Nat perks up. "It's busy. We got three double headers this week yet. You gonna come watch?"

Claude nods, "I'll be at your home games. I'm not going on the road with you guys though. My bones are a little too old to roam around and sit on bleachers. Sore butt."

Charlie holds up a hand toward Claude, "We're at the dinner table; we don't need to hear about your sore butt."

Nat laughs, "Speaking of sore, Coach is not going to be happy about my going to the basketball camps I got scheduled."

"Did you tell him already?" Charlie asks.

"I told him awhile back, but I think he forgot. I'll be back for the tournaments."

"Hey," Charlie frowns. "Tell him to get you a full-ride baseball scholarship, and maybe we can concentrate full-time on baseball."

Claude nods and points an affirmation-filled finger at Charlie while Nat laughs. "Nah, I'm stickin' with basketball," Nat shakes his head.

Charlie smiles broadly, beaming at his nephew. "Sounds good. Soon as we're done here, we'll meet on the driveway for a game of horse. You too, Dad."

Claude shakes his head, "You guys go. I'll handle the dishes."

*   *   *   *   *

The sun begins its descent, and the game of horse has evolved into a competitive one-on-one battle between Charlie and Nat. The whoops and hollers attract Claude from the sink to the living room window facing the driveway-court. Claude looks out the window and smiles as he holds a plastic Ziploc baggie, taking a break from storing the leftover chicken.

Chapter 8

Roberts County Standard

The Roberts County Standard is Sisseton's and the surrounding area's only newspaper. It is headquartered in Sisseton's central business district, a half-mile north off of South Dakota Highway 10, just past Brooks Motors, the Chevrolet dealership. The newspaper and its staff of two work out of a single story, non-descript building recording and reporting the local news. The Standard is owned and operated by Veronica Lewis. With the disappearance of Elliot Koffman approximately a year ago, there was a hole to fill in the community when Elliot's newspaper, the Chronicle, folded without him. As Elliot's right-hand person, it was only natural that Veronica stepped in to fill the void. She had done so admirably. With her sole employee, Susan, the pair manages a daily on-line edition of the newspaper along with a weekly edition for legal notices and to cater to the more traditional readers.

Veronica, a Fargo, North Dakota native, is a beautiful, dark-haired, wholesome, Nordic beauty, typical of the northern plains. At thirty five, she is a few years younger than Charlie, but they have been enjoying each others' company for the last year or so, ever since the nasty business with Elliot and the Deer Slayer. It was Charlie who had encouraged Veronica to go for it and dive in headfirst into the newspaper business. He hadn't realized how much time it would take away from their relationship, but seeing her happy was worth it.

The newspaper office is just on the edge of the historic downtown of Sisseton, with its one hundred year old brick buildings lining First Avenue East. The newer building had previously been home to an insurance agency and then a series of businesses called it home before Veronica rented the space for her newspaper. It is a hop, skip, and a jump from the Super Valu grocery store in one direction, and in the other direction, are the staples of a small town in South Dakota, hardware store, drug store, bakery, and bank. A few blocks away is the historic Roberts County Court House.

It seems slowly, but surely, the businesses are migrating from the central business district out to the main highway corridor of South Dakota Highway 10. Such was the case of Charlie's workplace, the BIA Police Station. It is a two or three minute trip for Charlie to navigate his BIA Police Tahoe to the ample street parking in front of The Standard's front door.

A smile turns up the corners of Charlie's mouth as he enters the newspaper office and sees the petite whirlwind bouncing between computers, typing a sentence here, then there, and shuffling through stacks of papers. Veronica looks up from the laptop she momentarily types on and gives Charlie a wave of acknowledgement.

Charlie stands by the door and observes the hectic situation for a few moments. "Are you ready?" he finally calls out.

Veronica looks up to see a grinning Charlie, arms folded, and leaning against the door frame. Her head goes down again, eyes focused on the screen. She sighs loudly, "Can you cut me a break? I'm trying to run a newspaper here!"

Charlie pushes off the door frame and shuffles toward Veronica. "This is a big one. First murder since Elliot." Charlie takes a precarious seat on the corner of her large government surplus desk.

Veronica stops her work a moment, furrows her brow, and frowns. She wags a finger at Charlie, "I've told you not to ever mention that name."

Charlie snickers, "Oh, yeah. Sorry. So, this is the first big story, a murder, since the name-who-shall-not-be-mentioned, skee-daddled out of town."

Veronica is finally able to crack a smile and chuckle. She stops what she is doing and focuses her attention on Charlie. Her brow furrows again. "Let me get this straight," she folds her hands together and extending her two index fingers, she touches her lips in thought. "Correct me if I'm wrong, an elderly man, a priest, is dead. You are saying foul play."

Charlie's head dips and his shoulders shrug, "Yeah, you can go ahead an' quote me on that."

Veronica follows up quickly, "Any suspects?" She reaches for her notepad and scribbles wildly, taking down Charlie's quote on a clean page as she waits for Charlie to answer her question.

Charlie shakes his head slowly, "You got my quote. That's all I can say."

Veronica grins up at her man a moment before putting her fingers back on the keyboard and typing, her eyes returning to the computer screen. "That's good enough for now. I'm doing the research. He seemed like he was quite the beloved, old priest. Who'd want to kill him?"

A radio in the back of the office produces a mellow tune, just above the threshold of hearing. J.D. Souther's "White Rhythm and Blues" fades away and a deep voice announces the title and artist. He continues his slow, breathy broadcast, "Here's another from J.D., John David Souther. A double play on this fine morning. This one is called, 'The Last in Love.' You may recognize it from George Strait's version that appeared in the movie 'Pure Country' several years ago."

Charlie stands and stretches as the music begins to play. He twists at the waist and, and his spine pops. "Uf-dah," he groans. He purses his lips and shakes his head while leaning down, kissing Veronica on the cheek. "Who'd want to kill a priest?" Charlie questions aloud. "It's a mystery. I'll see you tonight?"

Veronica shrugs while she types, "Tentatively."

Charlie cocks his head, "Whaddya mean?"

Veronica whines, "I'm working this story!"

"Give it to Susan," Charlie waves a hand of dismissal.

Veronica shakes her head, "Believe me, I thought about it. She's still too green."

"Fine. Let me know," Charlie mumbles as he turns and takes a step toward the door, but stops short. "Speaking of Susan, tell her I got her cooler."

"What?" Veronica flinches.

"Nat snagged her cooler," Charlie laughs the words. "We were fishing out at Buffalo Lake the other day."

Veronica is confused, "What are you talking about? Cooler?"

Charlie flips up his hands, "You know, her lunch cooler. A vinyl insulated container. It had a sandwich in it." Veronica's head tilts, still silently questioning. Charlie continues," She must have lost it out fishing. I've seen her out and about the lakes, fishin' from her canoe. Anyhoo, just let her know."

Veronica puts her hands in the air, "Just bring it in and leave it."

"No. I'll give it to her."

Veronica rolls her eyes, "Whatever."

Charlie leans down and kisses her again. "I gotta go. See you later."

"Bye," Veronica waves her fingers in a curl, before setting them back down on the keyboard.

Chapter 9

Five Alarm

Eden, South Dakota

Eden, South Dakota, population eighty one, is a paradise. Located in the heart of the Coteau Des Prairies, it is in the middle of a sportsman's paradise for hunters and fishermen. It is a typical rural town of its size with amenities such as a bar, a café, and for your agricultural chemical, anhydrous ammonia, and other fertilizer needs, a large lot that acts as an intermediate station where farmers can receive their supplies from a semi-truck. And one would be remiss to not mention the large Catholic Church. Eden is just off the Buffalo Lake District boundary of the Sisseton-Wahpeton Indian Reservation. The Buffalo Lake District is an important part of the commerce for the Eden community.

Religion, particularly Catholicism, plays a stabilizing role in Eden, boasting the over-sized St. Joseph Catholic Church. A slight overreach on the optimistic growth for the future population, the church's congregation never lived up to the imagined membership, but Eden residents, both Catholic and non-Catholic, are proud of the architecturally pleasing building.

An Achilles' heel of rural life is emergency services. A 2:00 a.m. blaze has no mercy, and tonight the victim of an arsonist is the historic St. Joseph Catholic Church. It was said later that the entire population witnessed the church burn to the ground. It was a five alarm fire. Eden's volunteer fire department may as well have been a bucket brigade in this malicious attack by a person intent on destruction. A gasoline induced blaze, five alarm fire, is no match for the part-time firefighters. It is a five alarm in that the surrounding communities of Roslyn, Webster, Britton, and Sisseton sent reinforcements of volunteer firefighters to assist in containing the flames to the church. Fear of losing every building in the community flared up with the flames off and on until the five fire departments were fully up and spraying water on surrounding trees and homes.

The sun did come up the next day, but to the residents of Eden, the hole in their community was as gaping, as the hole in their heart. It is a loss that could be the death blow to a small town. Gone is the soul of the social networking headquarters for the men, women, and children.

The morning is still. It is a rare summer's day without a breath of wind, and the column of smoke, hidden during the cover of darkness, now can be seen from miles away. Higher in the atmosphere, the winds buffet the smoke into a dark, gray cloud of surrender, shadowing the little town. As the sun rises, a majority of the residents are still on hand to not only encourage and thank the firefighters, but also to witness in first light, the scar left on their town.

*   *   *   *

Prior to the evening of devastation in Eden, Charlie and Veronica dine at the Dakota Sioux Connection. The casino restaurant is a regular routine for the couple. No cooking, no dishes, and all the convenience of a couple hands of black jack or a dollar or two in the slot machines for dessert. Maybe supper would be paid for that night. Just a short two minute drive from each of their offices, the Sisseton-Wahpeton Tribal casino, restaurant, and gas station is a thriving employment center for the tribe. It gathers the locals and the Interstate travelers with a strategic location at the interchange of Interstate 29 and South Dakota Highway 10.

The chicken strip special is the deal of the evening; Charlie selects the barbeque sauce, and Veronica prefers the sweet and sour, but sharing the flavors is the concept for the night. "Why didn't you invite Claude and Nat tonight?" Veronica's tone is slightly accusatorial.

Charlie sips from his soda, flinching at the question a little, "Hey, we need some alone time once in awhile."

"Oh, you're so sweet," Veronica blushes. "You staying at my place tonight?"

"That's the plan." Charlie nods.

Charlie points a finger toward the ceiling, country music from George Strait spills down in the form of his song, "Desperately" from the overhead speakers. It is barely audile. He smiles at his companion across the table. Veronica grins. The ringing of slot machines in the background competes valiantly against the background music, and the couple finishes supper only interrupted by their own casual conversation. On the way out the door, Charlie pauses, "I got five bucks. You want to see if we can get the tribe to pay for our meal?"

"Sure," Veronica shrugs and follows Charlie to the nearest slot machine.

Charlie loads a five dollar bill into the slot, and the machine accepts the deposit with a series of dings. "Here we go," Charlie mumbles. "A kiss for luck?"

Veronica kisses Charlie on the cheek. It is to no avail. In a minute and a half the credits are gone. "I guess we are donors tonight," Charlie declares.

"Aw shucks, maybe you can get lucky at home," Veronica bats her eyelashes.

Charlie rolls his eyes and puts his arm around her shoulder as they head for the door.

*   *   *   *

A restful night of sleep is not in order for the couple. Charlie's cell phone buzzes irritatingly on the night stand at 3:00 a.m., jolting him from a sound, release-driven slumber. Squinting against the grogginess of sleep, Charlie sees the caller id indicating it's Skip. "Hello," he hoarsely croaks.

Veronica, in her own fog of sleep, is not awakened by the phone buzzing, but she is roused by Charlie's voice, "What is it? Phone?" she whispers.

Charlie reaches a hand out to her naked body and strokes her hip, trying not to disturb her. The only illumination in the room is the digital clock and the screen of the phone lighting the side of Charlie's ear and hair in an eerie glow. Veronica is awake and pulls Charlie's hand to her lips, kissing his fingers. She can make out Charlie's other hand pinching the bridge of his nose as his eyes are clenched shut, the phone resting on the pillow next to his ear. The voice on the other end is squeaky-squawks, and she cannot decipher the conversation. Charlie listens silently, finally mumbling a deflating, "What?" into the phone, as he grabs the phone with his hand.

Veronica is up on an elbow now, trying to make out what Skip is saying. "Oh, no. Eden?" Charlie punctuates his few words with a heavy sigh. His head is nodding. "Jenkins. Got it."

Charlie ends the call and sets the phone on the nightstand before easing his head back to the pillow.

The curiosity is too much for Veronica; she shoves Charlie, "Well, what is it?" Her voice rises. "What happened?"

"The Catholic Church in Eden burned down. Skip suspects it was arson."

"What?" Veronica puzzles aloud.

"I know. That was my reaction," Charlie holds a forearm over his eyes as he reaches for the light on the night stand.

A surprised Veronica flinches, "Charlie! I'm naked! And you're blinding me!"

Charlie laughs as Veronica scrambles in the sheets. "I know. I wanted a last look."

Veronica gives a loving shove to her man next to her; Charlie takes the boost out of bed. "I gotta go."

Charlie slips on his boxers, watching Veronica watch him. He leans over and kisses her receiving lips, her one hand propping her up and one hand holding the bed sheet tightly to her chest.

"Burned to the ground," Charlie repeats the words slowly. "I guess they already got a suspect."

Charlie pulls on his socks and jeans. "Jenkins?" Veronica questions.

Charlie casts a suspicious glance toward her, "How did you know that?"

Veronica giggles, "I heard you say the name when you were on the phone."

Charlie points at Veronica, "You are not supposed to know that. Off the record!"

Veronica continues to laugh, "Fine. Just get going. I'm getting up too."

"What? Why?" Charlie questions.

"I'm going to have to cover this story!"

"It's in Marshall County!" Charlie argues.

Veronica is up and out of bed making her point. "This is a big story. It affects the reservation!"

Charlie points at her, "I can see you're naked."

"I know," Veronica says mockingly, "I'm giving you 'a last look' as you called it. Enjoy!"

Charlie smiles as Veronica makes her way to the bathroom. Charlie calls out behind her, "If you have to say something about the suspect, please don't use the name. Just say we have a suspect in custody!"

Veronica peeks around the corner already in a t-shirt and shorts. "How sweet of you. Where's this guy, Jenkins, from anyway?" Veronica approaches the bed and takes a seat, crossing her legs and kicking her foot impatiently. "Hurry up, finish getting dressed," she waves a hand at Charlie.

"Andrew Jenkins is the guy. He's from right there, the Buffalo Lake District. He's been screwed up for quite a while. Drug addled brain I assume." Charlie buttons his shirt.

Veronica cocks her head. "Don't worry. I won't mention anything other than you have a suspect. No names. I'm going to start this story, but probably hand it off to Susan."

"What if they are the same story?" Charlie locks eyes with Veronica.

Veronica's eyes widen, "You think?"

Charlie shakes his head, "First thing that popped into my mind. You got a dead priest," Charlie holds up one hand. "You got a Catholic Church burned to the ground," Charlie holds up his other hand. "Doesn't take much of a leap to connect the dots."

Charlie bends down and ties his boots. Veronica's eyes stare into the corner of the room as her mind processes the info. Charlie stands, leans down, and kisses her on the forehead. Veronica's attention is back to Charlie. She reaches for his head and pulls his lips to hers, "Be careful. Call me later."

"Will do," Charlie nods. He pulls away holding her hand and stretching their arms to full length before breaking away. "Bye."

"Bye," Veronica stands and follows Charlie to the door to lock the bolt.

Chapter 10

Diagnosis

BIA Police Headquarters – Sisseton, South Dakota

The Bureau of Indian Affairs Police Station located just off South Dakota Highway 10 and BIA Route 7 looks more like a bunker than a government building, because it is a bunker. Constructed in the early 1970's during the rise of the American Indian Movement (AIM), the sometimes violent Indian reservation protests prompted the federal government to build some infrastructure to serve as fortresses against trouble. That is an entire story in its own right that will be left for another day.

Charlie enters the police station through the secure back entrance after parking his BIA Police Tahoe in the fenced lot. The chain link fence and razor wire around the lot gives the building a cold institutional feel on the outside, and that stoic emotional presence is carried over into the architecture of the interior. The reinforced concrete walls and structural capacity have all the aesthetics of a 1950's Eastern Bloc country's buildings. Strictly functional is the theme. Charlie's footsteps echo down tile hallway in the early morning quiet, providing an almost foreboding that brings a smile to his face. In Charlie's mind the echoing "clop, clop, clop" of his boots foreshadowed something significant is going to happen, much like a special effects in a movie. Nonetheless, Charlie loves this old building that has been his second home for almost fifteen years. The main hallway forms a rectangle that serves every corner of the building. A person could do laps around this hallway and produce a workout of one-twentieth of a mile per lap.

As he approaches the front of the building, Charlie's footsteps alert Kathy Martin, the receptionist, at the helm this morning. The twenty-eight year old Kathy is already a ten-year veteran of the BIA Police.

Starting right out of high school, the five-foot tall tribal member with the bowling ball build, and wild hair is as dependable a worker as the day is long. Her bubbly personality is a welcome asset to all employees and visitors entering the building. Charlie can't help but grin as he catches a glimpse of Kathy's curly, billowing, 80's rocker hairstyle. "Mornin,' Charlie!" Kathy's sing-song voice calls out, echoing in the halls. "Skip wants to see ya."

She fumbles with the knob on her radio, turning down the volume on Ed Sheeran, who is belting out his tune, "Thinking Out Loud."

"Howdy, Kathy," Charlie beams back as he doesn't break stride, "That's where I'm heading"

Charlie continues past her desk and trudges on the polished tiles with a steady echoing-clomp of his boots. Three doorways down from Kathy, he arrives at the closed door with a nameplate indicating Captain Skyler Kipp. Charlie is puzzled. Skip's door is never closed. Charlie furrows his brow and looks back toward Kathy, considering whether he should inquire with her on why Skip's door is closed. He decides to go ahead and knock, rapping lightly on the door. Skip's voice, muffled by the door, calls out, "Come in."

The sterile theme of the police station continues in Skip's office. The gray concrete walls have seen several attempts to spruce up the mood, including the classic Animal House poster of John Belushi with his iconic black sweatshirt with white lettering indicating "COLLEGE." The poster now includes a customized photocopy of a BIA police badge taped to Belushi's chest. Whenever Charlie sees that poster, he always feels reassured that his boss is truly all that he is cracked up to be. With a quick glance around the room, and the poster drawing a hint of a grin, the sight before Charlie rapidly takes any air out of the room. Skip sits in his chair, elbows on the desk, and head firmly planted in his hands. Charlie is frozen at the door a moment, "Are you ok, Skip?"

Skip's body shakes and then heaves, the first sob emanates from Skip's chest, and Charlie hastily closes the door and approaches his boss and friend. "What's wrong?" He places a hand on Skip's shoulder in an attempt to comfort.

Between the whimpering cries that waver between sobs, Skip stutters the words, "I-I-It's Helen."

Skip attempts to gathers himself, but is unable to continue through his tears. Charlie's mind races at the pause. Charlie is sure, Helen, Skip's wife of almost thirty years and best friend since they were five years old, is dead. Skip manages to finally articulate the rest of his thought, "Sh-Sh-She's got the cancer."

Charlie, unconsciously holding his breath, gasps, and squeezes Skip's shoulder. "Oh, no." He pats his friend's back and scoots a chair close to Skip's desk and sits.

Skip is regaining his composure, and he pushes at his cheeks with the palms of his hands to squeegee tears away. "I need your help, Charlie. I don't know how to do this." Tears fall freely from his eyes, but the sobs and cries are now absent from his voice.

"I'm here for you, Buddy. Whatever you need," Charlie reassures.

Skip produces a handkerchief from his back pocket and blows his nose. "I'm sorry, Charlie. I'm such a mess."

"Don't worry about it. Whatever you need, just tell me."

Skip swallows with difficulty. "I'm going to have to take some time off. I hate to do this to you with the priest's murder and all, Charlie. You're going to have to pull some double duty as acting Captain."

"That is not a problem."

Skip shakes his head, "Jeremy will have to help pick up the slack. I know he's just a rookie, but he's been doing good. You keep workin' with him, show him the ropes like you been doin'. He's a quick study. Maybe we can get help from the Regional Office. They could detail someone."

Charlie waves his hands dismissing the request as not an issue. "Don't you worry about anything. You concentrate on taking care of Helen."

Skip draws a deep breath, "Thanks, Charlie."

"Don't mention it." Charlie smooths his hair uncomfortably. "Whatever you need."

The men are silent a few moments. Skip rubs his eyes trying to regain his composure. Charlie stands and puts a hand on his friend's shoulder. "I'll give you a few minutes, and then you and I will take a drive over to Eden."

Skip acknowledges his friend with a forced smile. Charlie pats Skip shoulder. "I dread seeing the damage. Think they'll rebuild?"

Skip scrunches his face and grimaces, "Yeah, you know the Catholic Church."

Charlie moves to the door, "All right." He reaches for the door knob. "I'll be in my unit. You come on out when you're ready."

Chapter 11

FBI

With Charlie behind the wheel of his Tahoe, handling the chauffer duties for the day, Skip enjoys a ride along. The men drive out of the parking lot onto South Dakota Highway 10, heading west, passing Valley View Country Club, up the Coteau, along the curving slope that parallels Long Hollow and its oak filled creek bottom. The conversation is light and airy, a far cry from this morning's heavy discussion. The men question the sanity of grown adults chasing a white ball around the golf course, and as Skip puts it, using finger quotes to emphasize the word "fun." The subject turns to the weather and the rains and how the fishing was so far this summer. Up on the top of the Coteau Des Prairie, the highway travels up and down little hills, snaking between sloughs and ponds, a bit of a challenge to drive, but much improved over the narrow highway with no shoulders just ten years ago. The South Dakota Department of Transportation has smoothed many of the hills and straightened all the sharp curves, as well as adding shoulders to the road, but it still feels like a fancy sports car would be a better suited vehicle to the banked turns of this stretch of highway.

The drive is cathartic. Even though Sisseton is a small town, every urban area has its oppressiveness, and on the top of the Coteau, the grind of daily life seems to melt away in the open air with only the scattered old farmsteads to remind one that you are still near civilization. Ten miles west of Sisseton, Charlie makes the turn onto BIA Route 3. Down a little bit of a grade and heading south then southwest, they pass Buffalo Lake and the tribal building for Buffalo Lake District. BIA Route 3 changes over to Marshall County 16 as they move off the reservation, and the men can see the smoke still rising from their position a few miles east of Eden.

The perfect late-June blue sky is a stark contrast to the charred skeleton of the church and parish residence. Skip and Charlie arrive to a bustling scene. Members of the Eden Volunteer Fire Department spray water and use long probing tools to hunt down hotspots amongst the smoldering beams and heaps of ash. Yellow crime scene tape encircles the entire city block. Skip and Charlie observe the devastation in stunned silence as their eyes squint, and they wince in the acrid air. The variable breezes waft clouds of smoke in and out of their faces.

Charlie's eyes roam, reluctant to comprehend the damage. He gives an elbow to his boss, "Look who's here."

Charlie points to a man looking way out of place, decked out in a fairly expensive suit and tie, leaning against a fire truck. The man stares blankly at the men spraying water in bursts. Both his hands are jammed deeply in his dark gray pants pockets. "Is that Agent Brown?" Skip questions. "Why is he here? This isn't the reservation."

Charlie shrugs. "Let's go talk to him and find out." Skip nods his head in the man's direction.

The sovereignty of Indian reservations produces an unusual echelon of law enforcement. The Federal Bureau of Investigation is the responsible party when it comes to high crimes on the reservation. State police, county sheriffs, and the BIA police force take a back seat to the FBI. Federal Bureau of Investigation Agent Austin Brown is a veteran agent covering South Dakota Indian reservations for the better part of the last seven years; his first and only assignment with the Bureau. At thirty five years old, Brown could pass for a younger version of Tommy Lee Jones. His rugged features and stern expression along with the "FBI uniform," a suit and tie, are dead giveaways of his profession. He's not flashy or arrogant. The steady business of crime on the reservations has brought Agent Brown to the Sisseton-Wahpeton Reservation, routinely providing him with a wealth of experience.

"Agent Brown!" Charlie shouts from a few yards away, "What's up?"

The agent turns with a surprised look on his face, not expecting to hear his name. He smiles a rare smile as he identifies the approaching men. "Sergeant LeBeau. Captain Kipp. What are you boys doing off the reservation?"

The men exchange firm handshakes of friends bonded in the brotherhood of law enforcement. Charlie laughs at the question, "We could ask you the same thing." Charlie gives a nod toward the smoldering ruins, "What gives?"

Brown points at the debris, mouth twisted in a grimace. "Take a look around. And you guys? What brings you guys by?"

"Just checking out the alleged handiwork of one of our tribal members," Charlie frowns.

Agent Brown nods, "So, I hear." He turns back to the blackened mess. "What a shame. How old was this church? I thought I heard somebody say seventy years plus?'

Skip nods affirmatively, staring at the firemen. "I think so." He turns his eyes to the FBI agent. "An' you? What's the FBI's angle?"

Agent Brown purses his lips, "Start burning down churches, even one church, and you get the full attention of the federal government."

A yell resonates from the debris where the firemen are concentrating their effort on hotspots. Charlie, Skip, and Agent Brown all turn their attention to where the yell comes from. The water has stopped, and there is a bustling of activity along the far corner of what is left of the charred rectory. Charlie verbalizes the thoughts of all three men watching the hustling firefighters, "I wonder what's going on over there?"

Agent Brown, having returned to his position leaning against the fire truck, pushes himself to an upright position, "Let's go find out."

The men slowly make their way around puddles, mud, and debris as they move to the perimeter of the blackened rubble. They approach the gathered firemen as a volunteer treads cautiously through the soggy, charred waste and shifting debris. Cries of "be careful" ring out steadily from his fellow firefighters. Making his way to a round object, he scoops it up. His face loses color, and his mouth is twisted in disgust. Tip-toeing through the maze of fire-wrecked timbers, he returns to his brethren. The fireman huffs and puffs as he reaches the edge of the debris field where the others wait. He holds out the object for the observers to see. It is a skull, a child-sized skull. Groans of everyone echo, and the murmurs grow louder. "Uh-oh," Agent Brown mutters, summing up what his two law enforcement mates are thinking.

"Stop what you are doing! Don't touch anything else!" Agent Brown shouts. "We gotta get this crime scene secured!"

Chapter 12

Grave Situation

Eden, South Dakota

The burned out remains of the St. Joseph's Catholic Church have the appearance of an anthill from a distance, except the bustling insects are replaced with expert men and women in white coveralls. The FBI has flown in its expert evidence recovery team. Overnight and through the next day, men and women from all over the country descend upon the rural South Dakota village to sort out the evidence.

About twenty people in their white uniforms, now becoming soot-stained and scuffed by the charred debris, carefully comb the burn-pit for human remains. Numerous bones are recovered and shuttled on sterile-looking silver trays to a tent city a block away in the Eden City Park.

Calling it a City Park is a stretch. Mature trees shading lush grass, two picnic tables, and two metal charcoal grills surrounded by several modern canvas tents fill up the park. Quiet generators hum a hundred feet away, providing power to the tent city.

Charlie and Agent Brown look over the shoulder of Dr. Keenan Salazar, FBI Medical Examiner, as he inspects the latest delivery of specimens. Dr. Salazar is a fifty year old graying, African American. He stoically sorts through the bones, assembling a skeleton of what appears to be a child. Oblivious to the men peering over his work, the doctor, clad in scrubs and gloves as if about to go into surgery, soldiers on with his grim duty.

"Number seven," Agent Brown mumbles. "Hey, Doc. Got a visitor. Dr. Salazar, this is Sergeant Charlie LeBeau of the BIA Police."

Dr. Salazar turns and gives a nod and a wave. "Pardon me for not shaking hands. Nice to meet you."

Charlie nods, "Hi, Doc."

The doctor returns his concentration to the bones. Charlie stands by Brown's side shaking his head. "I never imagined seeing anything like this in my life." Charlie looks around the tent filled with lab equipment that resembles a hospital operating room. Gesturing toward the door in the direction of the church, Charlie continues, "And those guys out there. It looks like an archeological dig of some sort."

Agent Brown nods, "Several of those men and women are archeologists. They have and use the same skills in trying to preserve all the details we might need. Photographs. Measurements. All the data and stuff to try to recreate what it was like before...before the incident."

Charlie takes a deep breath, "I just can't believe this." He manages a bit of a wry smile. "Must be nice to work for the FBI. One phone call and a day later you got FBI HQ, West."

Agent Brown holds up his palms and shrugs, "Hey, I tried to bring you on board, but no. You were content with the BIA."

Charlie waves away the comment. "If I'd joined the FBI, they woulda assigned me to who knows where. Probably New Jersey or other god forsaken place."

Agent Brown manages a laugh. "You are probably right. You are where you should be."

Charlie's eyes move across the tables taking in the partial skeletons of seven people, children. "Seven bodies. Uhg. All kids. It churns my stomach," Charlie puts a hand on his belly.

"Can you share anything with us, Doc?" Agent Brown throws a question to Dr. Salazar.

Without turning around, Dr. Salazar replies, "Looks like we got lucky in a lotta ways. A wall must have collapsed." The doctor holds up his left arm parallel to the ground and his right arm perpendicular to his left. He sweeps his right arm down like a windshield wiper atop his left. "The wall sandwiched the bodies, giving them some, well, quite a bit of protection from the fire."

Charlie and Agent Brown nod. "Cause of death is not clear. No trauma discovered yet," Dr. Salazar continues. "Found traces of lime and plastic burned and melted around the bones. It's interesting. They're saying it was likely a crawl space...the location of the bodies." Salazar shrugs. "Pretty much a standard 'm-o.' Bodies in plastic with some lime mixture buried in shallow graves. Seen it once, seen it a hundred times."

"Thanks, Doc," Agent Brown turns to Charlie. "You don't look so good. Come on. Let's get some fresh air and head over to my tent. Get away from this for a bit."

"You have your very own tent? Sheesh, what don't you have?" Charlie whines as Agent Brown leads him out of the doctor's tent.

"Let it go, Charlie. Let it go."

Outside the tent in the open, bright sky, the men take a moment for their eyes to adjust to the sun. The two walk slowly to the far end of the park, watching the recovery team work with survey equipment, cameras, and some heavy machinery to maneuver some beams out of the way. Agent Brown's tent is at the opposite end of the doc's mortuary tent. A robin sings in the tree overhead as the men leisurely amble toward the end tent. Agent Brown poses the loaded question to his friend, "What do you make of all this?"

Charlie shrugs and shakes his head, "Can't get my head around it yet. Makeshift graveyard, maybe?"

Brown scoffs, "Pretty naïve, even for you Charlie. I have a feeling it is much more sinister than that."

"What do you mean?" Charlie puzzles aloud.

"They're all kids," Agent Brown frowns. "All kids, about the same age, based on the size of the skeletons so far."

"I was thinking orphans," Charlie's eyes narrow. "Nobody to pay for funerals; the Church just buries them."

Agent Brown laughs disdainfully, "What? Do I have to spell it out for you? Catholic priests? Molestation scandal? You probably heard of it."

"Oh," Charlie flushes, embarrassed by his simple conclusions.

The pair arrives at Agent Brown's tent. He unzips the tent flaps, flipping them aside, "After you," Agent Brown sweeps his hand toward the interior.

Chapter 13

Missing Persons

"Step into my office," Agent Brown grins a cheesy smile as Charlie ducks his head and steps into the large canvas tent.

"Nice," Charlie comments with a little sarcasm in his voice as he looks around the space. Four folding tables, three stacked full of files, and the fourth sits empty with only a cup of coffee to support.

Agent Brown fixes the flaps open with Velcro straps. Sunlight pours into the tent, lessening the despondent, gray atmosphere. The tent gives Charlie a dank, prison-like feel. "Have a seat," Agent Brown points to a chair next to the empty table.

Charlie sits in a somewhat flimsy folding chair. Agent Brown grabs a file off the top stack from the closest table. He slides it in front of Charlie. "Go ahead. Take a look."

Charlie opens the file. An aged, black and white photo of a young Indian boy is clipped to an official, standardized form labeled "Missing Persons Report." Charlie looks up quizzically at the FBI agent.

Agent Brown taps the folder. "Missing kid reports from the area." The agent gestures toward the tables full of files. "I pulled case files from the region in a window of twenty to thirty years ago." Brown yanks a folding chair from the side of the table and sits down next to Charlie. "There are about sixty cases."

Charlie picks up the file and frowns as he looks at the photo of the smiling boy. He sets the folder down. His eyes narrow, and he turns his attention to Brown. "You think..."

Agent Brown cuts him off, "I don't think it. I know it." His index finger bounces firmly on folder, shaking the table. He is adamant, "The remains we're finding will have IDs in these files. I guarantee it."

Charlie's head shakes involuntarily, "I can't believe this."

"I don't want to believe it either, Charlie. But, that's just the way it is." Agent Brown is on his feet and sifting through more files. He brings four more back to the table.

Charlie closes the file in front of him and pushes it away. "I don't need to see anymore."

Brown sets the files on the corner of the table and sits down again. "Things can only stay buried for so long. Inevitably they surface. Like they said, it musta been a crawl space in the parish. Dirt floor under an addition. A sun room maybe."

Charlie nods, "The fire was so hot it cracked and heaved the adjacent basement slab. The water spray could have easily been the final push to unearth the bones in that dirt crawlspace."

Charlie contradicts himself and reaches for the files on the corner of the table. They are just out of reach, and Charlie wiggles his fingers as if psychically trying to draw them near. "Can I see 'em?"

"Are you sure?" Agent Brown questions.

"Yeah," Charlie nods.

Agent Brown hands over the files, and Charlie opens each file one at a time, only looking at the photos. "All young boys."

"Yup, all boys," Agent Brown softly mumbles the words.

"These kids would be my age now," Charlie shakes his head. "I don't recognize any of 'em off the top of my head. It's been a long time though."

Agent Brown stands. "We need the names of priests that used that house as a residence."

"That's an easy one," Charlie frowns. "I can give you one right now, Father Michael Franzen."

"Excellent," Agent Brown subconsciously adjusts his shoulder-holstered pistol hidden under his suit coat. "Let's go have a talk with the padre."

Charlie can't stifle his snort of a laugh. "You can talk to him all you want, but he's not gonna talk back."

Agent Brown cocks his head and furrows his brow as he considers Charlie's statement. "I see you already forgot about Skip giving you a call the other day. The dead guy on the reservation." Charlie pauses to see if it registers with the agent. "Before the burned up church."

"Oh, yeah," Agent Brown slaps a hand to his forehead.

Charlie smiles, "We pulled the priest's body from Buffalo Lake the other day. In front of his retirement cabin, not ten miles from here, as the crow flies. Speaking of crows, birds and fish had gnawed on him a couple days before we found him."

"Suspicious death?" Agent Brown questions.

Charlie nods, "It wasn't immediately apparent, but yes."

"Hmmmm," Agent Brown mumbles.

Charlie stands and shrugs, "I'm guessing the coroner's gonna announce the cause of death was heart attack, but we pulled a slug from the wall through the bed's headboard. We also had evidence of a shot fired through the dock into the water."

"Somebody induced his heart attack," Agent Brown speaks the sentence in a clipped tone.

Charlie taps a finger on his lips, "That was my conclusion."

Agent Brown frowns and sighs, "Dead priest. Burnt down church. Sort of ties things together. Looks like we'll need to talk to Mr. Jenkins on another matter, besides the 'playing with matches' issue."

"It can't be a coincidence," Charlie shakes his head.

Chapter 14

Jeremy Two Crow

Jeremy Two Crow is young, just twenty two years old. The world is just opening up for him. This morning he rides in the Tahoe's passenger seat. He can't help but smile as he enjoys the beautiful summer day. His smile is infectious. Charlie glances over and cannot help but grin himself.

Life didn't always seem so rosy for Jeremy. He grew up in a housing project on the outskirts of the small community of Pine Ridge on the Pine Ridge Indian Reservation in southwestern South Dakota. Pine Ridge is in Shannon County, South Dakota, and of all the counties in the entire United States, Shannon County is the poorest, and Jeremy's family fell right into this demographic. To say that the Two Crow family was poor is an exaggeration. You would have to have some money to even register on the scale of being poor, and the Two Crows had nothing.

Jeremy's mother was fourteen when she gave birth to him. She was dead at sixteen, killed in a car crash as a passenger in a car with a drunk driver. It was not even a ripple in Jeremy's life. He was too young to even know his mother. All he knew was his grandmother, Grandma Jo, who cared for him. Even with nothing, Grandma Jo put Jeremy on a path that led him to his life in law enforcement. The type of poverty on the reservation typically follows the same circle for its residents, despair leads to alcohol and or drugs. Drugs and alcohol lead to an early death. But, some are able to break that cycle, and Jeremy did it. Being poor on the reservation is deadly; there is no doubt about that combination. But, it can also steel a person's resolve. Jeremy knew the reservation was not for him by the time he was five years old. Grandma Jo protected him. She was a mother hen assuring his education, shielding him from the drugs and alcohol. The rugged reservation environment toughened the athlete inside of Jeremy. He was a state champion wrestler in the eighth

69

grade at 105 pounds, repeating the feat his junior and senior years in high school in progressively heavier weight classes.

A couple of partial athletic scholarships came his way, but wrestling had lost Jeremy's interest. He was ready to move on with his life. Attending technical school in Wyoming produced a welding certificate, and Jeremy jumped into the workforce in Rapid City, South Dakota, welding for a machine shop. Jeremy figured there was more to life and stumbled across the police recruiting booth at the Pennington County Fair. This was it. A life in law enforcement seemed to offer what Jeremy wanted, a chance to make a difference, a peace officer. In his research, Jeremy came across the Bureau of Indian Affairs Police Academy. Finally, he knew what he would do: serve his people.

The BIA Police Academy in Roswell, New Mexico, opened up Jeremy's world. He'd never been more than a couple hundred miles from Pine Ridge, and now, now he was getting a feel of what life was like. It was life, not just an existence. Jeremy loved New Mexico. He couldn't believe his own feelings. Jeremy vowed he would be back to explore New Mexico and the rest of the country.

Five months after graduating at the top of his class, Jeremy now sits smiling next to Charlie. His crew-cut is the only trait that defies his native appearance. He's a little on the small size, a bit of a disadvantage when providing a police presence, but a useful tool for people to underestimate you, and challenge you. His wrestling skills translated well into his finely-tuned academy training. There is nobody he couldn't subdue in a physical confrontation.

"You doin' ok so far, Jeremy?" Charlie asks as they roll down Highway 10 from the BIA Police Station.

Jeremy is all smiles, "Good as I can expect. I didn't realize how much paperwork police work is though."

Charlie laughs as he signals to turn onto First Avenue and head north to downtown Sisseton. "You and me both, brother."

"I still got seven months on my probationary period, but so far no problems."

Charlie nods, "Well, I think you're doing a great job. I'm glad to hear that you got no problems on your end."

Jeremy frowns a moment. "There is one thing. I'm not getting back to see my grandma as much as I promised her."

"I hear ya," Charlie nods. "Time just rolls by. Everything else ok?"

"Yeah," Jeremy smiles again.

"I'm askin' because we're going to be relying on you more than ever with Skip out of the office." Charlie takes his eyes off Jeremy, and the view in the rear view mirror reveals an out of state Escalade following him. It is a little bit too close to ignore.

Jeremy heaves a sigh, "Poor guy. Just let me know what I need to do. I'll do whatever you need. Whatever I can do."

Charlie drives more slowly as he keeps an eye on the mirrors; the vehicle is tailing him. "Good news is you'll get a lot more overtime. Bad news is...more overtime."

Jeremy laughs, "How's that bad news?"

"Well," Charlie bites at the inside of cheek, "you'll be tired. You get tired and you can be vulnerable to mistakes." Charlie glances at Jeremy nodding in understanding. "It can be a real test. I definitely don't want you to get burned out."

Jeremy is not smiling as he nods, "I understand."

Charlie checks his mirrors. "I'm counting on you to let me know when you need a break."

"Will do," Jeremy assures.

Charlie turns east off First Avenue and then south at the next block, keeping an eye on the vehicle still following him. Jeremy is smiling again, shaking his head. "Heck, Charlie, I never dreamed I would get paid to carry a gun and spend most of my days driving around helping people. This is a dream job," Jeremy beams.

Charlie is looking in his mirror. He can't help but smile at Jeremy's enthusiasm. He turns his Tahoe again and meanders through a residential area encircling the block as the Escalade follows. "I'm glad to hear it," Charlie marks the words emphatically.

Charlie continues to zig-zag through Sisseton's residential area, making a turn at every block. The tail is glued to Charlie's bumper. Jeremy's brow is furrowed when he looks a Charlie, "Where are we going? I thought we were going to get coffee."

Jeremy looks over his shoulder and sees the Cadillac Escalade shadowing them. His hand instinctively drops to his holster. Charlie catches the movement from the corner of his eye. His hand reaches out to calm his partner. "This is what I'm talking about. We got a lesson for you. Calm down. Get his license."

Jeremy rattles the plate off, "Minnesota Plate, TRX 599."

"Ok, hold on," Charlie says calmly.

Charlie flips on the emergency lights atop his Tahoe and whips a u-turn mid-block. "He's turning around," Charlie announces.

"He's definitely following us," Jeremy adds, his voice shrill.

"I'm going to whip 'er around again. Hold on!" Charlie spins the steering wheel.

The Tahoe responds well and is quickly on the rear bumper of the Escalade. Charlie hits the siren. It blasts a loud "whoop-whoop." He hits the switch for the loudspeaker and speaks into the microphone, "Driver, stop your vehicle!"

The Escalade pulls to the curb and stops, and Charlie gives another order through the loudspeaker, "Driver, turn off your engine. Get out of your car! Place your hands on the vehicle."

Chapter 15

Mr. Orloski

The driver's door of the Escalade opens and a large, heavy-set man emerges from the vehicle, placing the palms of his hands on the driver's side rear window after closing the car door. He's dressed in khakis along with a polo shirt topped with a sports jacket. It's a fashion look that Charlie notes is out of place. Charlie gives a nod to Jeremy, and the men exit the Tahoe. With hands on their weapons, they approach the man. Jeremy hangs back, shielding himself behind the front tire of the passenger side, his eyes dart between the man and Charlie.

Charlie approaches the man as he calmly speaks, "Do you know why I pulled you over?"

Without a tinge of sarcasm the man answers with his own question, "Because you are the police?"

"You were following too close," Charlie nods to the man. "You may reach for your license."

The man reaches for his wallet in his trouser's pocket, pulls out his license, and hands it to Charlie. In the process, Charlie observes a shoulder holster and pistol underneath the man's sports jacket. "Mr. Vincent Orloski. I'm afraid we're going to have to ask you a few questions...at the station. But, first, I'll need you to hand me your weapon. Slowly, two fingers only. On the grip."

Vincent Orloski slumps at the words. He does as commanded. Orloski is a forty-eight year old man that looks like he is going on sixty-five. His frame is heavy and pear-shaped and along with his bushy mustache, the man resembles a walrus. He does not argue or resist. "Any other weapons?" Charlie asks.

"I have a knife," Orloski confesses.

Charlie frisks him and notices the deceptive strength of this man under his seemingly fleshy frame. Charlie finds the four-inch, folding Buck knife, the kind he uses himself for deer hunting. Charlie cuffs the man's hands behind his back. "Could you," Mr. Orloski's husky voice rumbles, "have your deputy drive my vehicle to the station? I don't want it towed. I'm sure this is just a misunderstanding."

Charlie begins to lead Orloski toward the Tahoe, and Orloski continues, "I'll answer your questions, and I'm sure I'll be on my way shortly."

"Lock the vehicle," Charlie yells to Jeremy. "I'll tell you what, Mr. Orloski. We won't tow your vehicle...yet. Answer our questions, and we'll give you a ride back to your truck...in a bit."

*   *   *   *

At the BIA Police Station, Jeremy observes Charlie and his detainee, Mr. Orloski, through the two-way glass mirror. Charlie works the conversation, or in this case, the lack thereof, as the men sit arms folded, staring at each other across the interrogation room's table.

"I can sit here all day," Charlie smiles, "but, the longer I sit here, the more inclined I am to have your vehicle towed and impounded. I'd say you'd be lookin' at two days before you got it back."

Vincent frowns. Charlie shakes his head and leans forward on the table. "I'll ask you again, what are you doing here in Sisseton following me, a policeman, around like you were hitched to my bumper?" Charlie asks the question and leans back before continuing, "Look at you. You are dressed, like what? A private investigator in a cheap detective novel? Khakis and a sports jacket? But, what I'm still trying to figure out is you in an Escalade with out-of-state plates. Why don't you just paint 'Hey, look at me!' on your vehicle? On top of it all, you are carrying a pistol and a knife. Help me understand this."

Jeremy can't help but laugh from the other side of the glass. He watches Orloski squirm another minute or two before the big man places his hands on the table, tenting his fingers together, he speaks. "Fine."

Charlie straightens in his chair, "I'm listening."

Vincent Orloski's soft mumbling makes Charlie listen intently. "I'm from Minneapolis. I work for some people who are looking to get something back."

"I see," Charlie nods and stares at the man as a long silence again settles on the room.

74

Vincent's frustration builds. "Listen, I'm sorry I was following too close. I'm desperate to find info for my boss. I thought I'd just tag along with you and see what might turn up."

"I see." Charlie repeats again before adding, "Is the something they want back money?"

Orloski turns his eyes away from Charlie, fixing them on the doorknob. In his mind, Orloski pictures himself walking over, turning the knob, and walking out the door. He can see himself getting in his Cadillac and heading down the road. After two minutes he snaps his head back to meet Charlie's gaze. "Franzen," Orloski spits the word. "All right? That what you want to know? I'm looking for Franzen. Can I leave now?"

Charlie's hand is on his head, scratching an itch and smoothing his hair when Orloski's words tinged with anger spill forth. Charlie is frozen for a moment, hand oddly on his hair. He cocks his head, finally dropping his hand and asking, "A priest owes your boss money?"

"Yes," Orloski shrugs. It's a lie, but Orloski figures this story about money will get him out of the interrogation room.

Charlie stifles the urge to laugh, but can't hold back the smile as he asks, "Why would a retired priest need money from someone like your boss, a loan shark?"

"I don't ask questions. I just do what my boss tells me, and he said go collect the money."

"How much money we talkin' about here?" Charlie queries.

Orloski shrugs as he thinks about revealing a number. With just a bit of hesitation he shares an amount that he thinks would make sense. "Thirty thousand."

Charlie whistles in surprise at hearing the number. "You do know he's dead?"

Orloski' frowns, "The priest, Franzen? Yeah."

Charlie chortles at Orloski's forced response. He watches Orloski raise both hands in a shrug, "I'm still trying to figure it out myself, Chief. Or is it Sheriff?" Vincent Orloski squints at Charlie's name plate on his pocket. "LeBeau. Sheriff? Chief LeBeau? No offense. I mean as in Chief of Police, not as in Indian."

"It's actually Sergeant LeBeau," Charlie repeats softly, nodding in understanding.

"I'm very confused lately, Sergeant," Orloski shakes his head, "but I follow orders from the boss. He wanted answers. He wanted his money. I told 'em, 'Hard to get money from a dead man.' He didn't want to listen. He's got his own ideas." Vincent flips his hand up in the air in disgust ending his statement with a frown and a sigh. "Nonetheless, here I am, in Sisseton. 'Til they tell me to come back."

Charlie nods in understanding the man's frustration with upper management's decisions. "I don't want trouble," Charlie intones. "My advice to you is just go home. Father Franzen had a heart attack. He's not gonna pay. Tell your boss that's the price of doing business sometimes." Charlie stands. "You are free to go. I'll round up Jeremy. He'll get your belongings and give you a ride back to your truck. I hope you take my advice, and we don't see each other again."

Vincent smiles weakly. "Thank you, Sergeant LeBeau. I'll see what my boss says."

"Have a good day," Charlie says the words like it's an order. The interrogation room's door opens, and Jeremy is on the other side. "Officer Two Crow, can you please get Mr. Orloski his possessions and take him back to his truck?"

Jeremy nods, "Right away, Sergeant."

Chapter 16

American Legion Baseball

Charlie sits in the covered grandstand with Claude as they watch Nat play baseball for the American Legion-sponsored baseball team. In South Dakota a staple activity of summer for teenage boys is baseball. Fourteen to sixteen year old boys play in the Veterans of Foreign Wars, (VFW) sponsored baseball league. The sixteen to eighteen year olds play for the American Legion baseball league. The American Legion is a veterans' organization for men and women who have served in the military during a recognized conflict. Baseball is not a sanctioned South Dakota High School Activities Association event. School is not in session, and the youth baseball leagues are typically sponsored by a combination of the municipality and a non-profit organization, such as the Legion or the VFW.

In Sisseton the American Legion Post # 50 is called the Otto-Quande-Renville Lounge. Edward Otto, was the first casualty of the community in World War 1, Kenneth Quande, survived World War II's Bataan Death March, but not his imprisonment there, and Arden Renville, was a casualty of the Vietnam War. Each man is honored for their military service and memorialized by the Post as such. In addition to being a club for its members, the Post serves as a saloon where adults can come in and have a drink. It is also home of the Blackhawks drill team, a group that will often march for events to present the flag for the national anthem. Post # 50 in Sisseton sports a military tank decorating its parking lot just off South Dakota Highway 10. On the other side of Highway 10, the baseball field sits alongside the track and field complex. The aging grandstands are a throwback to the old days with compact, covered wooden stands. The sounds of the field echo through the wooden structure, and crowd noise is amplified like a megaphone pointed at the field.

Nat's Legion team competes against the Webster team tonight. The six o'clock sunlight bathes the field, highlighting the well manicured grounds. The grass infield is a little longer than usual, but the green grass, the red clay, and the white chalk provide a Norman Rockwell scene for spectators. Charlie and Claude sit about halfway up the bleachers, twenty rows behind, and just to the right of home plate, protected by the screen. From the third base access to the stands, Veronica and Susan appear. They spot Claude as he gives a wave for the pair to join them. The women make their way up the stairs and sit with the men. "Pulled yourself away from the paper?" Charlie teases Veronica.

Veronica smiles, "The news never stops. We got some big stories to cover."

Claude stands and extends his elbow to Susan. She grabs hold of his arm as she pulls herself up next to him. "Please excuse us," Claude bows a little toward Veronica. "We're going to grab some popcorn. Can we get you anything?"

Charlie and Veronica each hold up a hand and provide a simultaneous reply of "No, thank you." The departing couple waves and shuffles back down the steps and around the side of the grandstand to the concessions booth directly under the bleachers. Veronica and Charlie watch the pair disappear. Veronica smiles, "Aren't they a cute couple?"

Charlie's dismissive, "Yeah," brings a glare and a frown from Veronica. Charlie shrugs, "What? I said 'Yeah.'"

Veronica stares ahead. Changing the subject quickly, Charlie asks, "Anything new on our friend, the priest?"

Veronica rubs her nose. "Nada. We've kind of dropped that story, at least back-burnered it. We're looking at the stories of the families of the bodies they've identified so far."

The clank of the metal bat and the call of "foul ball" by the umpire rings through the stands. "They still have only two officially ID'ed as far as I know," Charlie mumbles as he watches the Sisseton batter hit a dribbler to the third baseman who tries to bare hand the ball, but fumbles it. A cheer and applause ripples through the hometown fans as they have their first baserunner of the game.

"Yeah, the two boys are the only ones they've figured out so far," Veronica purses her lips tightly, eyes welling a bit with tears as they discuss the sensitive subject. "They were in the social services system files; this is long before computers, mind you. Both were abandoned and in foster care. Wards of the state. The Church had pretty much defacto adopted them."

The catcher's mitt pops on each pitch to the Sisseton hitters, and Charlie watches the game action as he listens to Veronica. "Off the record," Charlie stares at the field, "Agent Brown told me I was naïve to not think this was a church related scandal."

Veronica agrees, "Evidence sure points that way. Did you happen to know these kids? They were about your age, huh?"

"Those names don't ring a bell with me," Charlie shakes his head. "I was in Catholic school only until third grade. My dad pulled me out to get, as he put it, a 'realistic' education." Charlie makes finger quotes on the word "realistic." He looks to Veronica a moment, then back to the field. "When I was out of high school, he told me that he didn't trust a couple of those priests."

Veronica's eyes meet Charlie's, and she nods in understanding. "Did you know Sister Susan?"

The crack of the bat clanks loudly, and Charlie, along with all the Sisseton fans, cheer and applaud as they plate their first run of the game on a line drive to the gap. "Sister Susan. Yeah, she was a nun when I was in school," Charlie nods in affirmation.

"She's my Susan now, you know," Veronica smiles. "She was telling me she quit the nun business about the same time your dad pulled you out of Catholic school."

"Hmmph," Charlie grunts. "I thought it was her, but I didn't want to say anything. Did she recognize me?"

"She didn't say. She wouldn't go into a lot of details," Veronica pulls at her hair.

Charlie smiles and nods as he watches the action on the field. "It's funny, she seemed familiar. That's thirty years ago. You can't fault either one of us for not recognizing each other."

"I kinda get the feeling your FBI guy is right," Veronica smooths her hair. "All this stuff is connected."

"Yup, you'll be wise to take the priest stuff off the back burner and try to follow that lead and see where it takes you." Charlie turns to Veronica again, brow furrowed, "Why is Susan here in Sisseton?"

"She has a sister in Claire City she's taking care of. Her brother-in-law died last year. You remember Bert Cox?"

"Yeah." Charlie points, "Hey, pay attention. Nat's up. Come on, Nat!"

The pitcher winds, and Nat takes a ball outside. The next pitch he lines back up the middle for a base hit. "Way to go, Nat!" Charlie yells.

Charlie looks back to Veronica, "You were saying something about Bert Cox?"

"Nothing," Veronica sighs. "Susan's sister was taking her husband's death pretty hard. She came to help out for a while. Listen, I gotta get back. It's going to be a real tear-jerker of a headline story this week. Two boys missing for thirty years...found dead. Good Lord." Veronica's eyes flutter as tears well up again.

Veronica stands. Charlie grabs her hand, "I'll see you later?"

Veronica winces, "No. It's going to be a late night."

Charlie stands and pulls Veronica close to him for a quick kiss. "Very well then. See you."

Veronica pulls away, "Call me before you go to bed."

Charlie nods and smiles, "Don't forget your assistant." Charlie tilts his head toward Claude and Susan standing behind the screen near the third base dugout, sharing a bag of popcorn.

Veronica rolls her eyes and giggles. "You better keep an eye on your dad. You can be their chaperone."

Charlie laughs.

Chapter 17

Fair Game

On the west side of Sisseton, just off Highway 10, the BIA Police Station compound sits adjacent to BIA Route 7, next to the old Viking Motel. Inside the station, Charlie is hunched at his desk in the shared area; short partitions form cubical walls providing faux separation from the work spaces of his fellow officers. He concentrates on the report in front of him, oblivious to his surroundings until he senses a presence, and a shadow looms over him, disturbing the illumination from the skylight overhead. Charlie looks up from the page, curious to the cause of his interruption. "Skip!" Charlie calls out, finding the source of the eclipse of his light.

"Hi, Charlie," Skip smiles meekly in seeing his friend.

"Sheesh," Charlie stands and grabs Skip's extended hand to shake it. "I hardly recognize you without your uniform." Skip laughs momentarily before heaving a weighty sigh. "So, how's Helen?"

Skip sighs again, "Treatments are brutal. But, doctors are optimistic."

Charlie nods, "Good. You all right? You want to sit?"

Skip waves away the offer, "That's fine. I'm just poppin' in for a moment."

"As you can see," Charlie points to the report on his desk, "I'm working away. Everything's under control. Don't worry."

"I'm sorry," Skip's head lolls to the side as he grimaces. "I sure didn't want to leave you hangin' with all this stuff."

"No, no," Charlie insists. "Don't worry about it. You just concentrate on your wife. Kids ok?"

"They're staying with my mom for awhile." Skip holds up a rosary and smiles. "Can you believe Helen wanted this?" Skip head bounces as he laughs scoffingly. He looks down at the beads, running them through his fingers. "With all this stuff going on, she still has the faith." He looks back up to Charlie. "This is the rosary she gave me when I was sworn into the force twenty plus years ago."

Charlie smiles and nods, "It's good to have faith."

Skip squeezes the rosary tightly in his hand, "She said it kept me safe all these years, now she wants it close to her for protection." He moves the rosary to his left hand extending his right hand. "I'll let you get back to it."

Charlie grips his friend's hand firmly. "You give Helen my best."

The handshake falls away, and Skip turns, shuffling off. Charlie's eyes note the sudden aging of the man he's called boss for over ten years. Skip moves into the hallway, and Charlie listens to the trudging steps disappearing down the hallway as he stares at the doorway.

Charlie turns his attention back to the report on his desk. He reaches for the papers and skims the information once again before tossing it back down on his computer keyboard. Marching out of the workspace and into the hallway, Charlie turns left, toward the front entrance and the receptionist's area. Charlie approaches the front doors of the entrance, glancing out to a passing vehicle on Highway 10. Kathy is perched at her administrative assistant's desk. Charlie smiles at the seemingly ever-present secretary, dispatcher, and jack-of-all trades when it comes to office operations. Kathy looks up from her desk, and her typically bubbly personality is all smiles. "Hi, Charlie! Did you see Skip? He looked like he was hanging in there. Did you get a chance to talk to him?" She speaks a mile-a-minute, and Charlie can't help but grin at the lovely lady in front of him. "I did see him. He said things are going ok."

"Did he already leave?" Kathy inquires.

"Yeah, he went out the back."

"Oh, bummer. I didn't get a chance to say goodbye." Kathy frowns momentarily before reverting to her bubbly self. "What are you up to today?"

"Not much," Charlie leans an elbow on the counter in front of her work area. "Have you seen Jeremy today?" he asks.

"Yeah, he came by and told me he was going out to do some traffic patrol."

"Oh, ok," Charlie raps his knuckle on the counter, "If you see him, tell him I want to talk to him."

"You want I should radio him?" Kathy inquires, starting to reach toward the radio.

"No, no. Just let him know I'm looking for him next time you see him." Kathy smiles, and Charlie turns away but quickly reverses himself to face Kathy again. "By the way, what do you know about the burglaries of the video games?" Charlie tilts his head back towards his office. "I've been reading the reports."

Kathy's expression turns to her frown again, her voice gets lower, and she speaks quietly, seriously, "Jeremy's been working on that. He mentioned that there have been four or five similar reports of stolen game systems. Playstations. Nintendos." Kathy leans closer toward Charlie, "Jeremy was very upset about it. He's a gamer himself."

Charlie raps his knuckles down on the counter, and Kathy flinches back in her chair. She smiles as she catches herself relaxing from the tension in her explanation. "Ok," Charlie points a finger at Kathy, "thanks."

"You're welcome," Kathy beams.

Charlie pivots and heads down the hall, back toward his desk. His mind swims with all that is going on, the church, the priest, and Skip. Now add to the pile a strange string of burglaries. Charlie shakes his head and whispers to himself, "There'll be no fishing for awhile, it looks like."

Chapter 18

Back to School

Charlie points his Tahoe west on Highway 10, he is heading back to Eden to meet with Agent Brown. The FBI man called to say he had a lot of new information that he would like to share. Charlie, tired of sitting at his desk, is much obliged for a road trip. The FM radio's country music with Dan Seals and Marie Osmond singing about "Meeting in Montana" fades from his mind as the highway hypnotizes Charlie almost instantly. His mind wanders back to his Catholic school days.

Charlie is eight years old. It is afternoon recess on the playground outside St. Ann's Catholic School. St. Ann's Church and school sit on the south side of Sisseton, surrounded by rows of mature blue spruce trees. It is a veritable oasis in the heart of the reservation. Charlie's brow furrows as he tries to recall the events he thought he would never forget, but, he realizes today, as he passes forty years old, memories fade and blur.

What he does remember is a very vivid picture of his tormenter, Ernie Azure. Ernie was eleven years old repeating second grade, repeating another grade as he had done with first grade and kindergarten in the previous years. Ernie is a husky kid with anger issues and, not surprisingly, learning limitations. He is a member of the Sisseton-Wahpeton Tribe, now in the care of his maternal grandmother who is unable to control him.

Charlie is oblivious to his drive as he climbs the Coteau and winds along South Dakota Highway 10 at the speed limit. Charlie's thoughts go deeper into his school days.

The grade-schooler Charlie was caught off guard when suddenly he found himself on the seat of his pants, shoved to the ground by Ernie. Charlie remembers the conversation and the malice in the bully's voice as he sat on the ground near the swing set, looking up at the angry boy. Ernie yells a question at Charlie, "Why were you talking to my sister?"

Some of the other kids stop what they are doing and observe, but most are used to Ernie's antics and don't bother to pay him any heed. Charlie moves to a kneeling position and brushes off the back of his pants. His eyes narrow and he looks up at the boy standing over him. "She was talking to me, and we don't need your permission to talk."

Two lackey friends, one on each side of Ernie, encourage his wrath with sarcastic "ooh's" and "ahs." Charlie remembers what a strange trio this was. Every kid had a blue denim jacket in those days. These three had matching denim jackets, but they were black. As Charlie thinks back on it now, he thinks of gang affiliations, and this was maybe the first time he ever encountered it.

Charlie starts to get to his feet, and Ernie steps forward, "Stay dow…" Ernie can't finish his command. Charlie sidesteps Ernie's casual effort, and the bully is off balance. Charlie finishes the job assisting Ernie's momentum with a push to the ground, finishing the humiliation with a swift kick to the sprawling boy's butt.

The kids on the playground are all watching now. "Pick on somebody your own size," Charlie yells down to Ernie.

Ernie is fuming. He pushes himself off the ground and begins chasing after Charlie. Charlie is ready. He has the advantage of quickness over the brute. He dodges in and out of the swing set's stanchion, grabs onto the supporting bar, and reverses course right into the charging bully. Ernie is caught by surprise and the chase is over in an instant. Charlie buries his shoulder into Ernie's soft belly. The momentum of the bigger boy carries the pair forward in a slow arc, ending with Ernie slammed on his back, knocked out of wind.

Charlie gathers himself, admiring his work as he stands. A full smile creases his face as he looks down at the gasping and crying boy. His joyful satisfaction is short-lived as he feels a pinch and a pull on his ear; he is suddenly being dragged toward the school building, Sister Selma, the crotchety old nun got him. "Come with me, boy," the nun hisses.

Chapter 19

Reckoning

Charlie knows he's in trouble now. Sister Selma is the meanest nun in the school. The stories he's heard about her adeptness with a wooden ruler are legendary. He had heard the older students joke about her graduating to the use of a yardstick, because she became bored with the limited damage a tiny wooden ruler could do to a disrespectful child's knuckles. Sister Selma was stooped-shouldered on her way to becoming a full-fledged hunchback. Her wrinkled face is frightening enough, but to be in her clutches is total defeat for Charlie.

Then it happened. Out of nowhere she appeared. As if an angel descended from heaven to intervene on Charlie's behalf. It is Sister Susan. The beautiful young nun watched the whole act play out and intercepts Sister Selma and Charlie. Forcefully, commandingly, she steps forward, "I'll take this one. You help Ernie."

Sister Selma and Charlie are both caught by surprise, but Sister Susan's commanding presence is spellbindingly authoritative. Sister Selma lets go of Charlie's ear with a nod and moves toward the boy writhing on the ground.

Susan is beautiful, radiant as she smiles down at Charlie. He is mesmerized and walks toward the school building, directed by Susan's hand on his shoulder. She is new this year. Charlie had seen her but never really noticed her. He gratefully notes her presence now. The pair puts some distance between the playground and the students staring and pointing at the still suffering Ernie. With a comfortable cushion of safety, Susan whispers to Charlie, "I saw everything, Charlie. Don't worry, you're not in trouble. We will go talk to Father Franzen before Sister Selma can bring Ernie along."

Charlie looks up in awe at his rescuer, barely able to nod at his good fortune. His wide-eyed, blank expression slowly turns to a smile as he realizes the truth; he is not facing a punishment. The trip to the principal's office turns into a relaxing walk for Charlie, and he begins to question the nun, "Where are you from?"

"I'm originally from Kansas."

Charlie nods, "I'm from here, well, Sisseton."

"Mmm-hmm," Sister Susan responds.

"Why'd you come here?" Charlie continues his interrogation.

"This is where I was assigned."

"Oh," Charlie opens the door for the woman. "Did you want to come here?"

"Thank you." The nun enters the building. "The Church needed me here, so I came here."

Sister Susan smiles and once again puts a hand on Charlie's shoulder to direct him. In a few steps they are outside the closed door marked "Principal's Office." Sister Susan looks down at Charlie. Her expression has become serious. "I will do all the talking."

Charlie nods, and Sister Susan knocks on the door. Charlie can hear a muffled voice from the other side of the door, "One moment."

They wait outside the door in silence a minute before the door opens and a young priest appears. He is dressed in a priest's traditional wardrobe, black slacks and black shirt, accentuated by the clergy collar. It is a young Father Franzen, and he emerges from his office with a young boy in tow, hand in hand. "Oh, hello, Sister Susan. You need to see me?" Father Franzen smiles, glancing from the nun and then to Charlie before turning his attention to the boy at his side, "Back to your classroom, Henry." The priest gives the child a pat on the back, sending him down the hallway. Charlie gives a smile and a wave to Henry Crawford, his classmate, as he passes by. Henry does not respond or even make eye contact, and Charlie turns his head, watching the boy walk quickly toward his classroom, eventually breaking into a run before rounding a corner in the hallway and disappearing. Charlie is puzzled. He looks quizzically at the adults looming over him. They are already in mid-discussion as Charlie begins to listen to the conversation.

"There was a bit of a scuffle," Sister Susan places a hand on Charlie's shoulder, "out on the playground, and I wanted to make sure Charlie was ok." Sister Susan sighs knowingly, "Sister Selma is bringing in the instigator." The nun heaves another sigh, "It's Ernie again."

For the first time, Charlie senses how dark it is in the brick school building. Having come from outside in the bright sunlight into the gloomy, dank hallway, he is surprisingly chilled. It is confusing for Charlie. He was fine and mesmerized by Sister Susan on the walk from the playground to the office, but inside he doesn't feel right.

Father Franzen is all smiles. "Very well, Sister," he looks back and forth between Susan and Charlie, and with a wink he proclaims, "I reckon I will await their arrival." Bending down the priest looks at Charlie and extending a hand, he tousles his hair. "Why don't you go on and head to the classroom to keep Henry company until recess is over."

Charlie shakes his head in agreement, eyes narrowing. His head hurts, not from injury but the confusing situation and the his adrenaline wearing off. He turns and makes his way down the hallway, the same as Henry had done.

*   *   *   *

Nearly twenty miles pass before Charlie is even aware he is driving. That odd feeling of "how did I get here" grips him momentarily. His memories of elementary school are not crystal clear, but they are still very vivid. He turns south off of Highway 10 and onto South Dakota Highway 25. He navigates the movement with no other vehicles on the road, and in a couple miles he passes Roy Lake and then the highway guides him between Stink Lakes. Seven miles after turning off Highway 10, Charlie is in Eden.

Chapter 20

Solved

Eden, South Dakota

Charlie arrives at the tent city that still occupies Eden's City Park. He parks and makes the short walk to Agent Brown's canvas abode. The flaps of the tent are tied open, and Charlie can see the FBI agent sitting at a folding table, working on a laptop. Agent Brown feels the presence as he breaks his concentration from the screen; he turns to the tent opening and sees Charlie, greeting him with a smile. "About time," Agent Brown chides Sergeant LeBeau with just a hint of playful sarcasm.

Charlie smiles, "I'm sorry."

"Let me show you something." Agent Brown gestures to a folding chair, "Have a seat."

Charlie moves inside the tent, grabs the chair, and places it next to the FBI man. He sits as Agent Brown clicks away on this computer, finally opening a video on the laptop. The grainy, black and white security video plays, and Brown turns the computer so Charlie has a better view. The video shows Andrew Jenkins filling up two five-gallon containers at the Holiday Gas Station in Sisseton. "Hmmph," Charlie grunts.

Agent Brown smiles and shakes his head, "Solved this one in record time. I showed Mr. Jenkins the video, and he confessed. Wrote it all up. Claims he was abused." He picks a manila folder up from the table, but sets it back down.

"Hate to say it," Charlie frowns, "but I'm kinda glad he burned this place down. We're going to have some closure for some families now." Charlie eyes the folder and nods his head toward it, "How about our other case? That it?"

Agent Brown puts his hand on the folder, "When you say 'other case,' I'm assuming you mean the priest." He picks up the folder, "We

scooped up his body in order to expedite the autopsy. We got 'er done."
Brown hands the folder to Charlie.

Charlie takes hold of the file and flips it open, extracting a one page
summary. He reads three paragraphs as Agent Brown watches him
silently. Behind the summary, fastened with a paper clip, Charlie looks at
two close-up photos of the victim's ear. He finishes his review and looks
up at Brown, who says, "Long story short, you were right. Father Franzen
died of natural causes...heart attack. All the blood work reinforced the
conclusion. However, we still got the photos."

"Yeah, the photos," Charlie nods.

"You're a pro, Charlie Le Beau," Agent Brown shrugs. "The Medical
Examiner hadn't even noticed until I paid them a visit. It's funny; they
calculated that the body was floating in the water 46.2 hours...however
they do that. Even with all that time in the water, they were able to
photograph that ear with special, filtered lenses and still see the powder
burns."

"So, I guess," Charlie hands the folder back to the agent, "we're all on
the same page here. Somebody scared the guy to death."

Charlie is about to say something, but Brown cuts him off, holding up
a hand, "I know what you're thinking. Could it be? Maybe? Possibly,
could it be our very own Andrew Jenkins?" Agent Brown snaps his fingers
and frowns, "Shucks, if it were only so simple. Alas, his window of
opportunity was closed according to the time frames we're working with.
He was in the Indian Health Services Hospital in Sisseton for four
days...alcohol poisoning. He's a long time abuser."

Charlie scoffs, "Abuser? That's the understatement of the year. I'm
not sure how that guy is even alive."

"Either way," the FBI Agent shrugs, "Jenkins is not our guy for direct
involvement in the priest's death, but were still looking at his friends and
associates." Agent Brown leans back in his chair, interlocking his fingers
behind his head. Relaxed and smiling he continues, "I think we got 'er
solved. Did some checkin' on Father Michael Franzen; turns out his
assignment here corresponds to the kids' disappearances. Open and shut,
now that he's dead. Makes our work easy."

Charlie cocks his head and frowns, "Still have the question regarding
who might have wanted to expedite Father Franzen's meeting his
maker?"

Agent Brown's eyebrows raise, "Do you really want to poke that
bear? Could stir up a lot of hard feelings. He died of a heart attack,
maybe we should just leave it at that. What is there to gain?"

Charlie chuckles, "I'm surprised. That doesn't sound like a federal agent talking."

"I'm just saying," Brown holds up his hands defensively. "Picking the scab off an old...no, ancient wound, doesn't seem to make a lot of sense."

Charlie cocks his head, "You Catholic, Agent Brown?"

Agent Brown bellows with laughter, "Hardly. Raised Lutheran, wife is Presbyterian. She takes the kids to church. I quietly abstain except maybe for Easter and Christmas." Brown laughs again. "Charlie, why do you always call me Agent Brown? We've known each other, what, almost ten years now? You can call me Austin."

Charlie smiles and nods, "Off duty. I'll call you Austin when we are off duty." He stands and moves to the tent opening looking outside for a moment. He faces Brown. His smile has disappeared. "I was kind of Catholic. This priest, Father Franzen. He was principal of St. Ann's Catholic School, so he was my principal and my priest when I was a kid."

Agent Brown's eyes widen and his jaw drops, "Did he..."

Brown doesn't get a chance to finish his question. Charlie cuts him off, "Nah." Charlie purses his lips and shakes his head, "I didn't understand it. I was in second grade, I think. Second or third grade. I didn't understand it at the time, but I'm sure my dad knew what was going on. I knew something was up. I'm almost positive, now that I think about it. Pretty sure that I had two classmates that were his victims."

"Jesus, Charlie," Brown gasps, "I'm sorry."

Charlie waves away the apology. He stares over Brown's head. His gaze is on the back canvas wall of the tent, but his focus is on his memory. "It was a different time. You couldn't talk about the church like that. Sacrilege. People whispered, and a lot of people left the church, including my family. It was never explained to me at the time, but I was pulled out of St. Ann's and put into public school. I was a little upset, you know, I had to make new friends." Charlie shrugs. "I do owe my dad for that."

Agent Brown nods, "Well, we're not done. We'll keep working. We'll get these families something. If not justice, some closure at least."

Chapter 21

Gabriel

Eden, South Dakota

Charlie leaves Eden heading east, along Marshall County Road 16; his mind is still preoccupied with the discussion and case information exchanged between Agent Brown and himself. The county road turns into BIA Route 3 as it hits the reservation boundary, and soon Charlie is distracted by Buffalo Lake, lapping on each shoulder of the road, the highway threading through the high ground. He slows as he winds around the shores. He looks through the trees, checking for any boats on the lake, and maybe an indication that the bite has returned. There are a couple of boats on the water, but nothing to indicate that he should call home to tell Claude to get the fishing gear lined up.

Soon he's back on Highway 10 heading east, coasting down the highway, descending the Coteau, past the country club and into Sisseton. The drive is a relaxing exercise, and Charlie finds himself smiling as he takes in the view in front of him. He can see the green fields for miles from the elevated position of the Coteau. He passes the Nicollet Tower, a tourist attraction where, on a clear day, you can see into Minnesota and North Dakota from atop the 60 foot tower.

Finally into Sisseton, his smile is wiped from his face, and his blood pressure jumps. "What the heck is this?" Charlie practically shouts the words. On the north side of the highway, in the A&W Restaurant parking lot, he spots a familiar black Escalade. He can see the Minnesota plates. Charlie scoffs with a grunt but can't help but smile as he realizes he is talking out loud. He has noticed it is becoming a more frequent event, the fact that he finds himself carrying on an actual conversation, aloud with himself. "What is this guy doing here?" the conversation continues. Charlie whips his SUV into the parking lot with a maneuver out of his police academy training days. "I guess I'll find out," he growls pulling into a parking space two spaces away from the Escalade.

Charlie dons his BIA Police ball cap, exits his vehicle, and can hear the Escalade's engine running. It is a little warm and the tinted windows are rolled up. Charlie strolls around his truck toward the Escalade. Clouds race by overhead. The sun is blotted out one moment, then fully shining the next. Charlie notices the warmth of the afternoon as he raps his knuckles on the tinted, driver's side window. There is a long hesitation, and Charlie raises his hand to tap on the window, but before he can, the window begins to move. Charlie begins to speak, disgust in his voice, "Mr. Orlos..." Charlie cuts himself off as the window lowers, revealing a young man in the driver's seat, not Vincent Orloski as he expected. The young man sports dirty-blonde, slicked-back hair with cheeks and chin of matching blonde stubble. Cool air flows from the Escalade's window, and Charlie notices the young man is clad in a black t-shirt under a black leather sports jacket. Charlie frowns and looks away from the smirking man to the passenger seat. The hulking Vincent Orloski sits quietly. He makes eye contact with Charlie and shrugs.

The young man's lips purse in a smile as he watches a confused Charlie try to get a grasp of the situation. "Hello, Officer. Fine day, don't you think?" The driver speaks with a wide smile.

Charlie tips his cap and meets Mr. Orloski's gaze before addressing the driver. The young man smirks as he chews on a toothpick. "Yes, Sir. Nice day. License and registration please, and if you don't mind, proof of insurance."

The driver's eyes widen in surprise. "Excuse me?" he questions.

Charlie stares down at the man, and tersely with staccato voice command, "License. Registration. Proof of insurance."

The young man's eyes narrow, and he frowns, pointing to Orloski and then the glove box. Mr. Orloski springs into action opening the glove compartment and rummaging through its contents. The man shakes his head as he fishes his wallet from his inside jacket pocket. Charlie's eyes discreetly catch a holster and butt of a pistol under the young man's jacket. Orloski hands papers to the younger man, and the man hands the papers, along with his driver's license, to Charlie.

Charlie quietly studies the materials while the young man silently looks to Orloski. His body language gestures a question to his companion. Orloski's face puckers as he shrugs a silent response. The young man's attention is turned back to the police officer as Charlie speaks without looking up, "I assume you have a permit for your weapon, Gabriel."

Charlie continues to review the documents noting the Escalade is registered to Franzen, Inc., and the proof of insurance reflects the same information.

Gabe's swollen posture deflates as he ponders Charlie's question on the weapon. His mouth moves, but there are no words. He shakes his head and looks to Orloski then back to Charlie. "As a matter of fact…"

Charlie cuts off the flustered young man, "Mr. Franzen," Charlie locks his eyes on Gabe for a moment before looking to the passenger, "Mr. Orloski." Charlie hands the materials back to Gabe. "You boys mind yourself while you're in Sisseton. Mr. Gabriel Franzen, nice to meet you." Charlie points a finger at Orloski. "I hope you have a talk with your partner, Mr. Orloski. And as I advised you before, I suggest you go back to Minnesota. Good day."

Charlie tips his cap and turns away, shuffling backward to his police vehicle, keeping his eyes on the men. Gabe watches the policeman move away; he turns to Orloski beside him and with a shrug and a frown questions the big man, "What was that about?"

Chapter 22

Bad Habit

Sisseton, South Dakota

From the A&W parking lot, it's just a couple minutes to the downtown office of the Roberts County Standard Newspaper. Charlie arrives at his destination, parking on the street in front of the newspaper office. As he exits his vehicle and moseys slowly toward the building, his mind replays the events in the A&W parking lot. He's puzzled by Franzen and Orloski's presence. It doesn't make sense to him.

The newspaper's door chimes as Charlie enters the building. Veronica and Susan sit at opposite ends of the disheveled office. The computer keys clickety-clack as the women type on their respective computers. Charlie pauses near the doorway, smiling at the messy office. It looks like a tornado has passed through, papers strewn on every square inch of desk space. Veronica glances up for a moment to see who has entered the office. She sees Charlie, smiles, and offers a simple, "Hi." She returns her gaze to her computer screen as she continues to type a mile a minute. "One second."

The office's storefront is made up of several large window panes and the sun comes through, brightly illuminating the workspace. Charlie crosses the room and approaches the desk, smiling and shaking his head as he passes a desk full of old newspapers. He picks up a discarded A&W bag off the floor and crumples it, tossing it into a waste paper basket next to Veronica's side table. She finishes typing as Charlie sits on the corner of her desk. "Busy?" he asks with a smile.

"T-uh," Veronica clucks her tongue with an eye roll. "Obviously."

Charlie nods as he reaches for a scrap of paper on her desk, trying to read it. Veronica slaps his hand away playfully. "Get away from that."

Charlie snatches his hand back. "You have to wait and read it in the paper."

"Fine, I'll wait," Charlie laughs. "You look busy."

"Susan and I are doing five features this week. Full stories on each of the victims identified so far, including pictures of the families."

"Sounds serious," Charlie quips nonchalantly.

"Damn right, it's serious!" Veronica shouts and flinches instantly as she looks toward Susan. She shrinks in her chair, embarrassed by her swear. "Sorry, Susan!" she calls across the room.

Susan looks at Veronica, smiling and shaking her head. "I'm not a nun anymore. Stop apologizing all the time. I'm just a person. Like anybody else."

"Sorry," Veronica apologizes for apologizing. This elicits a hearty laugh from Charlie.

"Well, I for one, am looking forward to your articles," Charlie stands. He points to Susan. "You mind if I talk to your employee a minute?" he asks Veronica.

"No, go ahead," she smiles. "Anything the law wants, the law gets." She winks at Charlie who rolls his eyes and moves across the room to Susan's desk. He stops short of her desk, hat in hand, and smiles. "Hi, Susan. Can you come out to my vehicle with me? Just for a minute? I got something to return to you."

Susan nods holding up a finger, acknowledging the request. She types for another minute as Charlie moves to the door and waits. The delay isn't long, as she finishes her thought, tapping it out on the keyboard. The spry old lady is up from her desk and moving to the door.

Charlie opens the door for Susan and points down the street to his police vehicle. They walk thirty feet to the vehicle, and Charlie studies the aged lady standing before him. The long silence is broken by the woman. "What?" Susan's brow furrows.

Charlie smiles, "You remember me? First grade? Sister Susan?"

"Of course I do," Susan smiles. "You were a good student. Why? You didn't think I remembered?"

Charlie nods, "You never know. Funny how time goes by, hmm? And, it seems so weird. So out of context for me. You, not as a nun." Charlie points to her head, "Without your hat. And no crucifix around your neck."

Susan shakes her head, "Yup. I retired that habit, my 'hat' if you will. I don't look back on it. I don't regret leaving the order."

Charlie opens the back door of the Tahoe and withdraws the soft-side cooler. "Hey!" Susan exclaims. "Where'd you get my cooler? It fell out of the canoe a while back."

"My nephew snagged it out fishin' Buffalo Lake." Charlie begins to extend the cooler toward Susan

"Tell Nat 'thank you' from me," Susan reaches for the cooler.

Charlie pulls the cooler back. "Just a question before I give it back. Do you know what's in this cooler?"

Susan frowns a moment then laughs, "A soggy sandwich, I'm guessing."

Charlie starts to extend the cooler again, and Susan starts to reach out, but Charlie pulls it back. Susan sighs and puts her hands on her hips. "Care to guess again?" Charlie inquires.

Susan cocks her head and her brow furrows, deep creases in her forehead reveal her frustration. "I'm not sure what you mean."

Charlie fixes his gaze on the woman. He notes her casual appearance, clad in blue jeans and white t-shirt. Her shoulder length, mostly gray hair is clean and neat. Her wire-rim glasses give her a scholarly look. "Why do you have a box of .45 caliber cartridges in your lunch pail?"

Susan blushes, momentarily flustered. It is only for an instant, and she quickly smiles, "Oh, those," she laughs. "You can never be too careful. I got a permit." She shrugs, "A lady by herself needs protection. I wanna feel safe, and I do."

Charlie nods, "There's nothing wrong with that." Charlie hands over the cooler. "Just be careful. We have a lot of problems with guns on the reservation. I'd guess our statistics would bear out that guns are the most common item reported stolen out of anything on the rez."

Susan hooks the strap over her arm, "Don't worry about me, Charlie. I'm trained. I've had my pistol for a long time. Just about as long as I've been gone from the church, pushing a little over thirty years now."

Charlie and Susan stare each other down. Charlie's expressionless face is mirrored by the former nun. Charlie finally nods, yielding, "Tell Veronica I will call her." Charlie shuts the rear door and opens the driver's door of his vehicle.

Susan nods, "I will. Goodbye."

Chapter 23

Fermented

Lakeland Lanes - Sisseton, South Dakota

The last frame was bowled about four hours ago. Now the lanes are quiet, and the lounge is empty except for two customers and the bartender. The lights are low; the music is barely audible. The loudest sound is the ice in Gabe Franzen's empty glass as he swirls the cubes and sips the last drop of whiskey on the rocks from his tumbler. The sounds of Diamond Rio and "Finish What We Started" drift through the bar. Vincent Orloski shakes his head at the bartender as he sits next to Gabe who stares down at his empty glass and holds his hand up high pointing to his drink, trying to get the bartender's attention. Orloski shakes his head and slashes a finger across his throat to make sure the bartender knows they are done. Orloski speaks in a soothing voice, "Gabe, please, just let this go. This is a loser."

The bartender approaches and almost in a whisper announces, "Last call, gentlemen."

Orloski slides Gabe's glass to the bartender, "Thank you. We're done."

The low lights of the bar with a bluish tint are suddenly vanquished by the harsh lighting of the combination of overhead fluorescent and incandescent lights. The bartender is wiping down one of the eight tables, and Orloski alternates between watching him and keeping an eye on Gabe. Gabe sits on his barstool, hunched over, leaning his elbows on the bar. Orloski stands close to his partner. The bar is about fifteen feet long, sporting seven stools. The room is empty and pathetic looking. Orloski's eyes take in the room under the full lighting. He shakes his head, trying to figure out what he's doing here. Following orders, that's what the voice in the back of his head tells him. He watches Gabe. Gabe is now staring at the Hamm's Beer motion sign. The scene changes ever so slowly as a stream appears to be flowing. Next to the stream a canoe is on shore, and then a fire appears. Smoke seems to rise up as the scene slowly rotates by. Gabe is mesmerized, watching the scene scroll by, but soon his head lowers, and he is staring down at the bar in front of him.

Gabe sits stock still staring down at the ring of moisture left by his last drink. He is intoxicated. Vincent Orloski is all too familiar with this situation. "Come on, Gabe, let's go. They're trying to close down." He places a hand on Gabe's shoulder and applies a bit of pressure, trying to direct him away from the bar.

Gabe shrugs maliciously. "Get your hand off me," he growls like an animal, speech slurred. Gabe doesn't look up from the bar, he just continues to stare. "You know what? You go. You go back to the cities. I'll handle this."

A stone-cold sober Vincent cocks his head, "As inviting as that sounds, Gabe, you know I can't do that. Boss wants me here...with you."

Gabe turns his head, glaring at Orloski. He sways a bit on the barstool, having moved his head and upsetting his equilibrium. Orloski holds up a hand to assist Gabe if he begins to lean off the stool. Gabe points a finger sternly at Vincent, "I'm the boss out here in this Podunk town." Gabe pounds his fist on the bar as his voice rises, "You need to remember that! When we are out here, I'm the boss!"

The bartender pauses from wiping the table and looks toward the two men. Orloski makes eye contact with the bartender and holds up a hand to assure him everything is ok. Gabe continues his rant, "I'm going to find out who murdered my uncle!"

Vincent meets Gabe's eyes, and Gabe returns his stare to the bar in front of him. Vincent's voice is soothing, "We both were there in your dad's office. We both heard him. He told us to take a couple days. See if we find anything. If nothing turns up, he specifically ordered us not to stir things up."

Gabe is up off his barstool in a flash. The stool almost tips over, but remains standing, rocking back and forth as Gabe viciously jabs a finger in Vincent's chest. Vincent backs up, surprised by the confrontation. Gabe's voice is low and guttural, emanating between clenched teeth, "I'll decide when we are done here. My uncle was a man of God. He deserves respect. Justice." Orloski throws his hands up in surrender as he backs up. "I don't care what my dad said," Gabe continues as he repeatedly pokes his finger into Vincent's chest. "This was his brother, my uncle...a good man murdered."

Vincent heaves a sigh and finally mounts a verbal defense, "I know. I know, Gabe, but sometimes the past is better kept in the past."

The storm of rage wanes from Gabe, and his hand drops to his side. Gabe's eyes well with tears. The alcohol has fermented his emotions. Vincent gives a nod toward the bartender, wiping down another table. "Come on, let's let the man close. I'll drive you to the motel."

Vincent gently grabs Gabe's elbow and begins to lead the exasperated young man toward the door. Gabe rips his arm from the grasp, "I can walk fine!" he shouts as he staggers.

Chapter 24

The Reservation

Dakota Connection Restaurant – Sisseton, South Dakota

Charlie and Veronica sit at a table in the restaurant, enjoying supper and conversation. Classic country music plays in the background in the form of Freddy Fender's "Before the Next Teardrop Falls." The song fades and eases into another country tune from Diamond Rio's Greatest Hits Album, "Love a Little Stronger." Charlie glances up as the hostess escorts two guests past his table; it is Susan and Claude arms interlocked. "Dad?" Charlie calls out as his father passes.

Veronica looks up from her plate upon hearing Charlie's question. She sees her employee. "Susan?"

Claude, oblivious to the other restaurant patrons until he hears his name, pauses and looks back. Charlie wipes his mouth with a napkin, smiles up at his father, "What are you doing here?"

Claude with Susan still hooked on his arm, pulls her back to the table. He points a finger at Charlie, "Since the chef was out tonight, I thought I'd forage with my friend for some food at the casino. Lucky we didn't need a reservation; I'm hungry."

"Where's Nat?" Charlie asks.

"Milbank. They got a double header tonight," Claude flips his thumb in the general direction of east as he nods to the hostess. He pivots, pointing Susan toward an empty table. "Our table awaits." Claude winks and smiles at Charlie. "Don't wait up."

Charlie gives a wave to the couple as they move away. He turns to meet Veronica's eyes; he smiles wryly and rolls his eyes. "What's your problem?" Veronica laughs. "They're a cute couple.

*   *   *   *

Claude and Susan are seated by the hostess and given menus. They check the evening specials, and in a few moments a waitress brings glasses of water and takes their orders. "Thanks for inviting me to supper," Susan smiles and sips her water.

"The pleasure is all mine," Claude mirrors Susan, sipping his glass of water. "I thought I'd upgrade from ballpark food."

Susan shakes her head, "Hey, I don't know. You can't beat a hotdog while watching a baseball game."

Claude laughs, "You're right." He stares at the woman across the table from him, examining her delicate, but aging, skin. He notices the only tell-tale sign of getting older in her pretty features, the crow's feet around her eyes.

Susan becomes uncomfortable at the long look, "What?"

Claude leans forward, hands folded on the table. "So, I've been dying to ask you something."

Susan shrugs, "What? Go ahead and ask."

Claude cocks his head, "Do you remember me? And Charlie?" He lifts a finger from his clasped hands and points it in the direction of Veronica and Charlie, with a dip of his chin.

Susan glances at the couple, quickly turning back to Claude. "It's funny you should ask. I just spoke to Charlie about the old days. Obviously the answer is yes."

Claude leans back in his chair smiling, and shaking his head, "Thirty-odd years ago, no?"

Susan giggles and leans back in her chair, relaxing. Susan notices she had bent forward in her chair, "Please, you're not supposed to delve into how old a woman is."

Claude laughs, "I'm just saying."

"I know exactly what you're saying," Susan mock frowns. "Let's just say it's a long time ago."

Silence settles for a moment before Claude starts up again. "So, you left the nun business and got out of Sisseton? What happened?"

Susan's expression takes a serious tone, "I think you know what happened. Didn't you leave the church about that time?"

Claude's head nods almost imperceptibly, his mouth twists into a frown, "I was never one much for religion. My wife, on the other hand, God rest her soul..." Claude glances toward Charlie's and Veronica's table. "Sorry about this conversation, I don't want to make you uncomfortable."

"No, no," Susan dismisses the comment. "It's good to talk about difficult things."

Claude beams, gives another glance in the direction of Veronica and Charlie, "But, you're back now, workin' with the paper. Why did you come back?" Susan shrugs and Claude continues, "Not that I'm complainin'. Need more pretty women around here as far as I'm concerned." Claude winks at Susan and she blushes.

Susan looks around the room, taking in her surroundings. Her eyes move to the large bison head mounted on the wall. Next, she takes in a bison etching by local artist Paul War Cloud. The walls are dotted with other Native American memorabilia. She notes a handcrafted bow with arrows in a quiver hanging in a shadow box next to a warrior's traditional leather shirt with intricate beadwork and a line of leather fringe running the length of the sleeves. The lines in her forehead are revealed with her serious expression. "I left Sisseton sooner than I wanted. You know, with all the falling out with the Church, I couldn't stay. This is such a beautiful area. I wanted to enjoy the things I missed out on. You could say I had unfinished business."

Claude lifts his water glass in a toast, "Well, here's to finishing business."

Susan grips her glass, raises it, and clinks it off Claude's, and they drink. Setting her glass down, Susan folds her hands in front of her. "Tell me, what's it like to be an Indian?"

Claude leans forward laughing, "What's it like to be a woman?" he laughs the words.

Susan laughs, "I'm sorry, that was a weird question."

Claude smiles with a shrug of his shoulders, "That's all right. I get that question every once in a while, and it always cracks me up." He shrugs, "I've always been Indian, always will be an Indian. I don't know any different."

"I am so embarrassed," Susan turns her eyes down to the table and covers her face with her hand. "What a stupid question!"

"Don't worry about it," Claude waves his hand, trying to push away Susan's discomfort. "I think I know what you mean."

"I...I," Susan stammers a bit, "how do I say this? How are you different? How did you escape the poverty of the reservation? You and your family...you're just like any other American family. But...but a lot of Indians on the reservation, they don't seem..." Susan is unable to voice her thought.

"Vietnam," Claude answers succinctly.

"Vietnam?" Susan questions, flinching at the word.

Claude's face is painted with a dour expression. "The military. I saw the world. I was forced off the reservation by the draft. I didn't really want to go, but I saw that there was more to life than being tied to the reservation." He gives a nod toward Charlie across the restaurant. "Charlie saw it too. I encouraged him to enlist."

"But you're still on the reservation," Susan states flatly.

Claude's lips jut outward as he thinks a moment. "When I got out of the military, I got a job with the Bureau of Indian Affairs here on the rez. A good government job. I got married and needed to provide for my family."

"I just don't understand this culture," Susan throws her hands up and then refolds them.

"What's to understand? There are a lot of Indians on the reservation that have never been fifty miles from the house they grew up in."

"But, why?" Susan puzzles. "I don't understand what makes you or some of the others like you so different."

Claude shrugs and shakes his head. "I think a doctoral thesis or two, or a hundred have been written about that question." Claude rubs his chin. "I'll tell you what I think, based on my unscientific observations. I've always thought it was the reservation itself. The government told the Indians, 'Stay on the reservation, and we'll take care of you.'"

Claude laughs in disdain of his own comment. "Look around." He sweeps his hand around to his side. "This is what a failed socialism experiment looks like. Food stamps. Indian Health Service. Government housing. What's the incentive to do anything? People don't live on the reservation. They only exist."

Susan frowns and jabs the air with her open hand, pointing toward Claude. "But, I still don't get it. You broke away."

"I can only speak to what I've seen and lived. The military drafted me and gave me some perspective." Claude's face twists in pain, "Like I said, there's a lot of Indians that think the sun rises and sets only on the reservation. We tend to have a tight knit culture. It keeps people frozen in place, scared. I was lucky, I got out. By the grace of God, the military and the draft lottery called me and took me off the reservation."

"You got out, but here you are?"

Claude smiles, the darkness of his expression lifts. "Like you said, it's a beautiful place. What more do I need?" He extends his arms from his side and looks left then right.

The food is delivered by the waitress, and Susan digs into her fries. Claude holds up a finger. "One final thing that I'd say, and this is how the reservation and its people were explained to me one time." He lifts a French fry to his mouth and hesitates, "The reservation, it's like a big bucket full of crabs. Slowly a crab might move up, towards the top of the bucket, ever so close to escaping. But, just before the crab can get over the edge, a claw reaches out and back into the bucket, that crab is pulled."

Susan eats a couple more of her fries, then grabs another, pointing it at Claude. "You are quite the philosopher, Claude LeBeau. I should do a profile on you for the paper."

"Oh, please," Claude waves a hand at her. "Let's just eat."

John Arthur Martinez's version of "When You Say Nothing at All" emanates from the overhead speakers.

Chapter 25

The Boss

Sisseton, South Dakota

With every governmental agency there is paperwork. The Bureau of Indian Affairs Police Department was no exception. The morning had been productive for Charlie as he sat in his cubical. He had caught up on the week's case reports, timesheet approvals, and, most importantly, the mandatory crime statistical report required every other week. This report was typically done by Captain Kipp, but Charlie had inherited this duty for the time being. Skip had emphasized this report above everything else with a warning, "If you want all hell to break loose, just forget to email the stats. Believe me, I know from firsthand experience."

Charlie is staring at the final folder for his morning's review when he hears a familiar voice shout from the hallway, "I'm looking for the man in charge!"

Charlie looks up from the burglary file toward the doorway to the office space he shares with three other cubicles. Charlie has refused to move his work space to Captain Kipp's office so far, choosing to remain at his permanent work station among his fellow patrol officers. He recognizes the voice as FBI Agent Brown, but his usual low key vocals sound boisterous, a little foreign for his personality. "Where's the boss?" the agent bellows.

Entering the doorway, Brown halts and leans on the frame, holding up a brown accordion folder strapped tightly shut with an elastic band. "There you are," the agent beams. He holds the folder eye-high and twists his wrists, presenting the package with a magician's flourish. Charlie pulls out a chair and pushes it toward Brown. "Skip's still out, I hear."

Charlie nods in affirmation, "With his wife in Rochester."

Brown pulls up the chair next to Charlie and sits. "No matter, I'm here to see you anyway." The agent leans forward and flips the folder onto Charlie's cluttered desk with a thud. "There you go," he smiles.

"What did you bring me?" Charlie questions, eyes narrowing, "And why are you so upbeat? This isn't like you."

Agent Brown smiles and points a finger at Charlie, "It's not what I got, it's what *you* got...now. You are welcome in advance." Charlie shakes his head in silence, puzzled by the cryptic speech and dramatics. "You're gonna love me," Brown giggles. He points a finger at the folder on the desk. "It's your Deer Slayer. He's alive and well."

Charlie's eyes widen as he tentatively reaches for the file. "Are you messing with me?" Charlie frowns, cocking his head and glaring at the agent.

"No, Sir. I flagged a lot of financial files that we recovered at Elliot's house. One came back this week with activity. The computer boys said it's an offshore account."

"Whoa," Charlie gasps.

"First blip on the radar in over a year," Brown smiles. "That's all we got right now and not much we can do, but we'll keep our ears to the ground. But, he doesn't know that we know, if you catch my drift." He gives Charlie a wink.

Charlie sits in stunned silence at the news. He nods and smiles reflecting the agent's wide grin. "In other news, Boss, got some more info on your dead priest."

Charlie's grin disappears, and he holds up a halting hand, "Please, I'm not the boss."

Agent Brown shakes his head in disagreement, "Sure you are. No Skip means you're the man now."

Charlie sighs, "What do you got?"

"You're gonna love this. Our dead priest has a brother in the Twin Cities. The Franzen name came up early and often in the organized crime unit's computer records."

"Hmmph," Charlie grunts.

"What's with you?" Brown frowns. "I thought you'd be surprised."

Charlie sighs, leans back in his chair, and folds his arms. "I've already had a run in with the Franzen family. Gabe was...is in town."

"Ah, I see," Brown purses his lips. "Yeah, that's the priest's nephew. He's a very bad boy. He's already done some time for conspiracy. Took the rap for his pop."

Charlie's eyes narrow with a question, "Why would they be so keen on a child-molesting uncle?"

Agent Brown shrugs, "Family is family. Blood is thicker than water. Yada, yada, yada. These families can't show any sign of weakness. Somebody messes with your family, you gotta respond."

From the hallway a voice rings out, "Charlie." Through the door Jeremy Two Crow appears. He's looking down at a piece of paper. When he looks up he sees Charlie and the FBI agent looking at him. "Oh, sorry. I didn't know anybody was here."

Charlie and Agent Brown stand. Charlie steps forward, "No problem. Jeremy Two Crow, this is FBI Agent Austin Brown."

Jeremy and Brown shake hands. "Nice to meet you," Jeremy nods.

"Likewise," Brown responds.

"He's our rookie," Charlie points at Jeremy while giving a knowing grin to Brown.

"I'm sure you'll break him in right," Brown smirks.

Jeremy laughs uncomfortably, "I'll come back and talk to you later. Nice to meet you." Jeremy exits quickly.

"Nothing like new blood," Agent Brown nods.

"He's a good one," Charlie nods. "Back to Franzen though. Do you think his family even knows?"

"Knows what?"

"That their favorite old Uncle Mike was a pedophile?"

Agent Brown folds his arms and shrugs, "Probably not."

Charlie sighs, "Well, this is great. I get to deal with a mobbed up punk kid bent on avenging the murder of his favorite child molesting uncle...and we don't even have a suspect."

Agent Brown bursts out laughing, "What are you complaining about? This is an easy one. When you find the next dead guy on the rez, you can pretty much figure he was the priest's murderer. And, you'll already have your next suspect, the nephew. Piece of cake!"

Charlie laughs and shakes his head. "If only it was that simple."

"Have a good time," Brown edges toward the door. "I'm outta here."

"Where you going?" Charlie queries.

"I'm heading back to Pierre for a few days with the family. I'll be back next week to shutter the field investigation in Eden." Brown throws a salute with a smirk to Charlie. "See you, Boss."

Charlie smiles and returns the salute. "See you later."

Chapter 26

Jimmee Turquoise

Roberts County Standard Newspaper Office

The job never ends if you're the manager of a small town newspaper. Veronica frets over the layout table, shifting advertisements and stories to model and make the best use of space. Susan sits near the front window engrossed in her story about the upcoming county fair. The door chimes, alerting the office occupants. It is Claude entering the building and remaining near the front door. He announces clearly, "I'm here to call on Miss Montgomery." Susan looks up from her computer and waves to the man at the door. "Care to take a stroll down the street?"

Susan looks to Veronica, "You mind?"

Veronica does not even look up, "Go ahead. Take a break."

Outside on Sisseton's First Avenue, Claude and Susan stroll north on the sidewalk, moving uphill at a snail's pace. "Thank you for dinner the other night," Susan breaks the silence.

"The pleasure was definitely mine," Claude responds.

They walk in silence a few more moments before Susan initiates the conversation again, "I thought a lot about what we discussed that night."

Claude nods as they pass the bakery; sniffing deeply, he inhales the scent of fresh bread. "Mmmm, gotta love that smell." Claude glances at his companion. "Sorry, I don't mean to get distracted. What about our discussion intrigued you?"

"I'd like to profile you in the paper, remember? I was serious. People would like to read it."

"I don't know about that," Claude scoffs."

"I think it would be a wonderful story, and you would have your philosophy recorded for all time."

The conversation goes quiet as they soldier uphill, passing a boarded up store front. Claude gestures toward the building, "This used to be part of the Stavig Brother's store. They were the biggest merchants within a hundred miles. They lasted, oh, I don't know, fifty plus years. Things change. It's sad in some respects that now all we have is just a big, empty building. It's hardly a blip in history for those immigrant brothers. But, we still got the Stavig House as a museum."

"The store was open when I was here the first time, but that was thirty years ago," Susan notes. "But, more importantly, listen to yourself. You're a natural philosopher-historian."

"You should have seen the bakery, even fifteen years ago," Claude turns back momentarily and gestures toward the bakery behind them. "Back then we would have to make our way through a line of people out the door at this time of the morning. Things change."

They pass the drug store with the ancient Rexall sign still hanging in place, coming to the Cherry Street intersection. "Shall we cross to the shady side of the street?"

Susan nods and extends her arm, interlocking elbows with her escort. They mosey across the street. In the cool shade on this warm summer morning, the couple approaches an elderly Indian man leaning against the corner of the hardware store's brick wall. He is Jimmee Turquoise. His face is rough with the scars of acne and psoriasis. The bulbous nose of an alcoholic dominates his face. His exposed skin is bright red. The man's long, formerly black hair, is mostly gray now. The seventy year old man looks more like he's in his mid-nineties.

"La-boo," Jimmee grunts, "can you spot me a dollar?"

Claude reaches into his pocket and extracts some currency. "Sure, Jimmee. Here's two. Get something to eat."

Jimmee nods and pockets the cash in the chest pocket of his faded denim jacket. "Thanks, La-Boo."

"Anytime, Jimmee Turquoise. You have a good day."

Jimmee holds up his index finger and intones, "Every day alive is a good day."

Claude and Susan move along down the street. "What's his story?" Susan asks. "I've given him money, but I've never asked him anything."

Claude clucks his tongue, "Tsk, tsk, tsk. And you call yourself a reporter."

Susan laughs, "Technically, I never went to journalism school. I'm a teacher by trade. Come on, tell me about him."

"Well," Claude begins, "Jimmee Turquoise was a classmate of mine in high school. Did you notice his turquoise rings? That's how he got his name. Jimmee Gray Stone is his real name. Most don't even know that. I'm guessing the average person in Sisseton looks at him the way they look at a stray dog. They just want him to stay away."

"I saw the rings," Susan pipes up, "very beautiful."

"Of all the things he's pawned in his life," Claude continues, "you'd never find him without those turquoise rings."

The couple stops walking at a gap in the central business district. A building lost to a fire a few years ago is now a city owned "open space." This means that the empty lot was paved and two picnic tables, one with a canopy, were placed on concrete slabs. To the east you can catch a glimpse of the top of the county court house. In every other direction, you can take in the heart of Sisseton's commerce. They sit at the covered picnic table, and Claude continues. "Jimmee spends most of his time right here. He has a house, umm, about three miles over," Claude points to the southeast. "Over by the IHS hospital. He goes there to sleep sometimes when it's cold or to clean up. Most nights, Charlie and his crew will put him in the jail."

"He's got a house?" Susan questions, surprised by the information. "I just figured he was homeless."

"No, he's got a house," Claude nods his head. "He just chooses to let his kids and grandkids stay there. He doesn't want his alcoholism to dominate their lives too."

"I see," Susan affirms with a nod. "He's a very generous man."

Claude's head bobs in agreement. "To tell you the truth, I am amazed he's alive, as much abuse as he put himself through." Claude looks far away to the west and the Coteau. He shakes his head. "The reservation. I remember talking to one of my BIA co-workers thirty years ago. Larry McDonald, a white guy. He was a civil engineer in the BIA roads department." Claude snorts a single laugh. "We had an intense conversation about the reservation, and he said something to me about the reservation that I've never forgotten."

Claude's eyes meet Susan's eyes for a moment before he looks back to the rising hills in the west. Claude shakes his head. "He told me that the reservation 'is a blight on the Indian people.'" Claude's mouth twists into a grimace. "That's how he started the conversation." Claude half smiles. "He said 'it's an unintended consequence of sympathetic Christians, mostly the Catholic Church.' Empathy. Pshhh," Claude groans.

Susan gasps, "Really?"

Claude's eyes remain focused on the far off horizon. "Yeah, as Larry put it, 'never had a conquered people not been wiped out, enslaved, or forced to assimilate in the history of the world's wars.'"

"Hmmm," Susan ponders the thought.

"I tend to agree with him. Think about it," Claude continues, his voice going higher. "Religion stepped in and influenced the government to round up the poor 'savages' and set them aside on a reservation. Keep the Indians and white men separate, and everything will be fine! How abstract of a concept is that?" Susan frowns and shakes her head. Claude's thoughts pour out, "Larry's words struck me like a lightning bolt. I thought he was right on the money. Nail on the head. What he was saying was so true, but it had never even occurred to me."

Susan speaks one word as she nods, "Assimilation."

Claude meets Susan's eyes, "You can see what the reservation has done for my people. Look around. I struggled with Larry's characterization of a 'conquered people', but he's right. You either get wiped out in war, or you surrender and sue for peace. Indians were on the brink of being wiped out and negotiated all kinds of treaties." Claude shrugs, "Can't go back in time."

Claude's eyes drop to the concrete under their feet. Susan places her hand on his shoulder. His eyes move to the corner where Jimmee stands. "Larry was a pretty astute guy," Claude's voice wavers a bit. "It still puts a lump in my throat, the one final thing he said on the subject. And we never discussed it again. He talked about the Black population, the slaves in this country. They had an Emancipation Proclamation and a Civil War that made them free." Claude's eyes well with tears. "Indians are never going to get that freedom. We're enslaved to the reservation for eternity."

Susan's hand runs down from the emotional man's shoulder. She clasps his hand, trying to provide some comfort. Claude inhales a deep, shuddering breath and heaves a sigh, "It still makes me sad."

Chapter 27

Fuel

Holiday Gas Station, Sisseton, South Dakota

On the east side of Sisseton there sits a landmark of the region, the Holiday Gas Station. The gas station has been in operation along the south side of South Dakota Highway 10 for almost seventy years. The business's road sign is faded, after sitting in place for thirty years; the red, white, and blue colors have yielded to the elements, however the business inside thrives. For Charlie, the Holiday Station has been around longer than he has been alive. He can still envision his formative years as a child, tagging along with his dad to fill the truck with gas and stop at the square-shack of a building to pay and pick up any odds and ends a person might need. From a box of shotgun shells to a carton of milk, from Quaker oats to a giant pickle sitting in a huge jar near the register, the little gas station seemed to have everything. Just the name "Holiday" had a special ring to it for a young Charlie. It was a special occasion to go get gas and a treat.

Forty years later the modern building with convenience store and coffee shop is a far cry from its original setup, but it is still a special place for the community. Charlie and Veronica sit in a booth of the coffee shop, enjoying a hot beverage in the bustling store. In addition to providing fuel, gasoline for the cars, and coffee and snacks to boost the customers' energy, the Holiday Station coffee shop also provides the fuel for gossip in the community.

Charlie sips at his Styrofoam cup full of piping hot, black coffee. "I had quite the enlightening conversation with the FBI this morning."

Veronica's eyebrows arch, "Oh, really?"

"You remember how I mentioned that if you had some time, you could Google search Gabriel Franzen?"

"Yes, I remember," Veronica rolls her eyes. Her voice is defensive, "Sheesh, I'm sorry. I'm kinda busy running a newspaper."

Charlie holds up a hand to thwart the rebuff from Veronica. "No, that's not what I meant," he laughs. "Agent Brown gave me the rundown on the Franzen family. Gabe is connected."

Veronica's eyebrows pinch together. "Connected to what?"

Charlie leans in and whispers, "Organized crime." Veronica's eyes widen as Charlie takes a quick glance around the room to see if anyone is listening. He continues in a hushed tone, "It looks like Father Franzen, who had no ties to the family business, was Gabe's favorite uncle."

Veronica's eyes roll again, and her voice is thick with sarcasm, "Let me guess; Gabe wants revenge."

Charlie raises a hand and pinches the bridge of his nose between his finger and thumb. He closes his eyes for a moment. "Tshh, yeah, the guy is still hanging around town with his partner." Charlie opens his eyes and meet's Veronica's again. "I get the feeling this whole case is going to cause me some headaches."

Veronica reaches across the table and places her hand on Charlie's, gently patting it, "As painful as this all is, just think about the tiny piece of closure it brought for all these families. Almost forty years of wondering what happened to their son or brother, finally, people know. Don't know why, but they know their relative's fate." Charlie nods in agreement. She squeezes his hand. "Hey, don't forget we got that concert this weekend."

Charlie manages a smile, "I haven't forgotten."

The owner of the Holiday Station, Marvin Hattum, sidles up to their table. Marvin is a husky man, a gentle giant. He is almost as wide as he is tall, a looming presence. The fifty-four year old, gray-haired man smiles down at the couple. "What are you two love birds up to?"

Charlie quickly yanks his hand out from under Veronica's. "Hi, Marv," Charlie blushes guiltily. "Looks like you're trimming down. How much you lost?"

Marvin beams proudly, "I've lost thirty pounds so far. Thirty to go. Feelin' good. Should be ready for this deer season. Can't wait." Marvin talks a mile a minute; his excitement is uncontainable. "I already got some trail-camera photos." He jabs a thumb over his shoulder toward the massive deer mounted on the wall. It sports a large, symmetrical rack of antlers, seven on one side, eight on the other. "Got a photo of one that could be this one's twin." Marvin leans to the side and stands on one leg. "My foot's all healed!"

Charlie smiles up at the man, "That's great. Glad to hear it." Charlie gives Marvin a wink. "I'm guessin' you didn't come over to chat about deer huntin'; you got any gossip for us?"

Marvin leans down. He looks around the store nervously, checking out the other customers a moment before whispering, "Mob's in town. I seen 'em."

Charlie catches Veronica's eye and frowns knowingly. "Really?"

Marvin leans closer, "I'm assuming it's the casino business. I heard something 'bout that."

Charlie's head bobs in understanding. "Thanks for the info," he speaks earnestly. "I'll keep an eye out."

Marvin looks nervously around the coffee shop. He holds a finger to his lips. Charlie nods and mirrors the gesture, glancing to Veronica. She mimics the "sworn to secrecy" signal. Marvin backs away with a wave, returning to his post at the cash register.

Charlie and Veronica snicker. "I shouldn't laugh," Charlie shrugs. "Maybe he's right, and I'm wrong."

Veronica smirks. "Out here on the reservation, who knows? You're probably both right."

Chapter 28

Brass Casings

Bureau of Indian Affairs Police Facility - Sisseton, South Dakota

As Charlie walks the hallway toward the front desk, the rookie officer, Jeremy Two Crow, calls out, "Charlie, wait up." Charlie pauses and turns to see Jeremy loping down the hallway, boots clomping on the tile floor as he hustles to catch up. The young policeman waves a folder in his hand as he approaches, finally handing the papers to Charlie as they fall in stride walking toward the front of the building. "Agent Brown left these with me." Jeremy smiles as Charlie opens the folder and glances at the papers as they walk. "He said he forgot to leave them. It's the ballistics report on the slugs taken from the priest's cabin." Charlie casts an eye toward Jeremy and then back to the papers. Jeremy shrugs a guilt-ridden shrug. "Sorry, I looked."

Charlie closes the folder. "That's ok. Can you just give me the summary?" Charlie stops walking and faces Jeremy. "Sure," Jeremy halts and taps the folder with a finger. "The slugs were too deformed and mangled to get any lands and grooves information." Charlie nods and Jeremy continues, "Interesting info about the brass. They did recover both casings. The report indicates the cartridges were fifty plus years old based on their oxidization. They tested the powder residue inside the casings and confirmed the gun powder formula of many years back. Finally, according to the report, the ejector signatures on the brass indicate a WW II Colt .45 Model 1911."

"Interesting. They can tell that from the brass?" Charlie puzzles aloud.

Jeremy nods, "That's what the report said."

"Hmm, interesting," Charlie's head continues to nod as he repeats himself.

"I know," Jeremy pipes up.

Charlie taps Jeremy on the chest with the folder appreciatively. "Thanks for the summary." He turns to continue his jaunt down the hall, but pauses. "How's the video game burglary case going?"

Jeremy has turned to head down the hallway, back to his office area, but now he stops and just stands facing away from Charlie. His muscles tighten, fists forming into balls as he turns to Charlie and speaks through gritted teeth. The words are angry, tipped with venom, "What's that supposed to mean?" Jeremy glares at his superior, frowning menacingly.

Charlie's head tilts as he tries to comprehend the young man's reaction. With a shrug, Charlie replies, "I'm just asking about the case." He holds up a hand, trying to calm Jeremy.

Jeremy relaxes as he realizes Charlie is not teasing him. The corners of his mouth twitch, reversing his frown into an embarrassed smile. "I thought you were messing with me," he laughs nervously as his anger dissipates. "We just got two more reports of stolen games and consoles last night."

Charlie shakes his head, "Oh, Geez. What the heck is goin' on out there?"

"I don't know, but it pisses me off," Jeremy gets worked up again, as he punches his balled up right hand into the palm of his left.

"Take it easy," Charlie smiles. "You going out to follow up on the reports?"

Jeremy nods and relaxes again. "Soon as I'm done talkin' to you," a smile crosses his lips.

"Well, don't let me hold you up," Charlie gives a wave toward the door.

"All right then," Jeremy nods. "See ya, Boss." Jeremy gives a casual salute, turns and quickly moves down the hall.

"Hey, Jeremy," Charlie calls out after the young man, halting him. "I know you'll get 'em."

Jeremy salutes again and hustles away.

Chapter 29

Super Valu

Super Valu Grocery Store – Sisseton, South Dakota

In the rural towns of the Midwest, the grocery store is an equalizer for all segments of the population. Everyone needs to eat, so, much like a trash collection contractor or the local mortuary, where people are dying to give you business, providing sustenance is steady work. The Super Valu grocery chain reaches across the Dakotas and Minnesota. With its modest buying power at the wholesale level and distribution points; it fills the rural niche market demand. With the arrival of the much more expansive Teal's Market at its South Dakota Highway 10 location, the Super Valu and its downtown location was slowly working its way into oblivion.

Super Valu is still old school in that it uses bag boys and bag girls to sack the groceries and haul them to your vehicle. That is the default scenario unless you intervene and demand to transport your own grocery bags. The position of bag boy/stock boy at Super Valu has initiated thousands of youngsters into the labor force. Nat Chasing Hawk is a member of the bag boy club, now in his third summer of work at Super Valu. He doesn't mind the work. In fact, he enjoys it. It is a constant stream of accomplishment as he sees it. Whether it is replenishing canned goods, dusting off the shelves, or hauling out sacks of groceries, Nat notes that you can always see your completion of a task.

Nat smiles as he bags the groceries for a familiar customer, Susan. With the money exchanged and a cartful of food, Nat follows Susan across the parking lot to her car. "You coming to my game tonight, Miss Montgomery?" Nat poses a friendly conversational question.

The cart rattles loudly over the rough parking lot as Susan nods her head and raises her voice over the cart's racket, "Probably, at least for a little while, a couple innings."

"We play Webster again." Nat frowns, "They're not very good."

"You going to pitch?" Susan queries.

"I think so," Nat rotates his shoulder. "At least a couple innings."

They approach Susan's car, and she pops the trunk with the remote button. Nat forges ahead, sidling up to the back end of the sedan with the cart. He lifts the half-opened trunk to get full access for placing the groceries. Nat does a double-take as he glances into the compartment. "Cool pistol!" he says as he notices the weapon resting atop a battered sweatshirt in the corner of the trunk. He reaches in the trunk and picks up the gun. "Grandpa Claude has one just like this." Nat's face crinkles, "Wait, this isn't his is it?"

In the blink of an eye, Susan reaches for the pistol, snatching it from the boy's hand and slapping his empty hand. Nat flinches back like a scolded puppy. "Don't you know better than to grab another person's weapon?" she scolds.

Nat recoils. He stares at his feet in shame. "I'm sorry. It's just that my grandpa…"

Susan cuts the boys apology short, interrupting with her own, "I'm sorry, Nat. I shouldn't have a gun out in the open like that. I usually keep it tucked away here in my purse." Susan jams the pistol down in her already bulging hand bag. "I'm sorry."

Nat shrugs as an awkward pause falls over the pair. Nat reacts by unloading the grocery sacks from the cart and carefully placing them in the trunk. "That's ok. I better hurry up," Nat remarks. "We're getting busy. You know how it is the tenth, eleventh, or twelfth of each month." Nat stows the last grocery bag and closes the trunk.

"No, what do you mean?" Susan asks with a puzzled look on her face.

"Food stamps come out," Nat states matter-of-factly. He swings the cart around, pointing it back toward the store. "Well, not exactly food stamps anymore," he continues. "The EBT cards get re-credited. You know, the Electronic Benefit Transfer cards."

"Oh," Susan nods.

"Yeah, we really get busy on those days, and it seems to be starting now," Nat gestures at several cars pulling into the parking lot. Nat pushes his cart back toward the store. "I'll see you tonight at the game." He waves and smiles at Susan.

Susan waves, "Sure thing, Nat. See you later."

Chapter 30

Clear Lake

An evening with no work and no baseball games finds Charlie, Nat, and Claude fishing. According to Claude, Clear Lake was this week's hot spot, so the rods and tackle are loaded in the truck, and a half hour later the lines are wet. They fish the State Park access area. The beach is weed free for the swimmers, but the adjacent flanks grow a healthy crop of aquatic foliage. Charlie and Claude watch their bobbers, while Nat casts a heavy lure to no avail.

Charlie was suspicious of Claude's scouting report on Clear Lake as soon as they pulled into the State Park boundary and could see the lake itself. Only two boats floated on the large lake. This was the first indication of a slow night, but Charlie held his tongue. An hour later with no action, Charlie is ready to comment on Claude's choice of lake, but his father beats him to the punch, "Nice night anyway."

Charlie smiles acknowledging his father's admission of fisherman's guilt. "Yeah, it's nice to have some peace and quiet. Seems like every evening now after supper, that phone won't stop ringing with recruiters."

Claude stares out at the bobbers and nods. Charlie watches his nephew cast his lure and reel it in quickly. Nat can overhear the conversation, and he smiles, glancing toward his uncle and grandfather. "It's nice to be wanted."

The wind has faded to nothing, and the lake is like glass, except for the ripples of Nat's lure splashing into the water. Charlie watches the tiny waves tickle the bobbers next to the weed bed. He turns his attention to Nat. "You leanin' towards any school yet?" he asks.

Without missing a beat, Nat has an answer, "Duke or Harvard, so far."

Both Charlie and Claude laugh with a snort. Charlie stares at Nat with a stoic expression, "I mean, the non-fiction version. You know, schools that actually might want you."

Nat laughs. "I know!" Nat casts his lure again. "Don't worry, Uncle Charlie, I'm staying small and close. I don't want to sit on the bench and wait. I'm only going where I'll play right away."

"Good. Good," Claude is in adamant agreement. "Stay close, and maybe we can come see you play."

Nat reels his line in quickly, in disgust. "I'm gettin' nothin' with this Daredevle. I'm gonna try a Rapala." Nat marches over to the tackle box near Charlie and Claude. He rummages through the lures, finds a blue and silver minnow-like lure, and clips it to his line.

Claude sighs, "So much for the radio report I heard. Nothin' bitin' tonight at all. Still nice to be out though."

Charlie turns the conversation back to Nat with a question, "Thought about what you might study?"

Nat casts his Rapala and lets it sit on the surface a few moments. He looks to Charlie. "I got a couple ideas."

"Care to share them?" Charlie inquires.

"You'll probably think they're lame." Nat flicks the tip of his rod, and the lure darts under water for a moment. He reels up the slack in his line and pauses.

"Why would you say that?" Charlie questions. "What do you have in mind?"

Nat reels his line, flicking the rod periodically. "You already know the one major I've talked about. Teaching, just like my mom. Coaching and teaching."

"Yeah," Charlie agrees. "What's the other one?"

"I'm on the school newspaper. After talking with Veronica and Susan, I've been thinking about journalism."

"Hmm," Claude shrugs. "Interesting."

Nat laughs, "I guess they've rubbed off on me." He casts his lure again.

"I'll bet," Charlie pipes up, "that if you talked to Veronica, she'd be happy to have you do some work for her. Get you some good experience. She's always busier than heck."

"Susan too," Claude adds. "She'd probably love to have you shadow her and do research."

Nat casts his Rapala again, perfectly nestling it alongside the weeds. He jerks the line and begins to retrieve the lure. "Speaking of Susan," Nat laughs. "Funny thing happened the other day at the grocery store." Nat pauses his retrieve of the lure. "I was hauling Susan's groceries to her car, she popped her trunk, and there was a pistol just like Grandpa's sittin' in the middle of the trunk."

Charlie's stare at his bobber snaps over to his nephew, his eyes narrowing. "Oh?"

Nat laughs and shakes his head as he reels in his line. "I picked up the gun and she had a fit."

"She had an Army-issue Colt, like Grandpa's?" Charlie points a finger at Claude.

Nat affirms his response with a nod, "Yeah, it was nice. Perfect condition, just like Grandpa's."

Charlie turns his attention back to his bobber. His mind churns over Nat's information, combined with the ballistics data Jeremy had provided earlier in the week.

Nat casts again and reels in his line. He shakes his head, "Pretty funny, huh?"

Charlie continues to gaze at the red and white float on the water. "Yeah, I need to have a chat with Susan about firearm safety, it sounds like."

Claude yawns and stretches. "What do think?" He looks at his watch. "Half hour more, and we can call it a night?"

Nat frowns, "Yeah, not even a single bite. Weird. Fifteen minutes and if we got nothin', let's go."

The sun begins to set, and the men enjoy the last orange reflections off the mirror-like surface of the lake.

Chapter 31

The Letter

Charlie's quiet morning finds him topping off his fuel tank on his BIA Police Tahoe. "Silence Is Golden" by the Tremeloes plays from speakers attached to the canopy overhead. His mind wanders as he watches the digital dollars and gallons race by on the pump's screen until his peripheral vision catches movement through the back window of the Tahoe. Charlie's posture straightens, and he stares through the vehicles tinted windows, trying to see who is on the other side of his vehicle. Mr. Orloski edges around the back of the vehicle, and Charlie sighs after subconsciously holding his breath. His hand drops from the handle of his pistol.

Orloski notices Charlie's hand drop and he smiles. "You got a minute?"

Charlie draws a deep breath, "Mr. Orloski...you know," Charlie pauses, "you shouldn't be sneaking around like that."

Mr. Orloski laughs, "Sorry about that. I was just easing up to talk to you, seeing who might be watching. Can we talk?"

The fuel shut off clicks on the nozzle, and Charlie squeezes a bit more gas into the tank. "Sure." Charlie returns the nozzle to the pump, replaces the gas cap, and points to the store. "You want some coffee?"

Orloski points to the Tahoe. "I was just thinkin' we could talk in your truck. Private."

"All right then," Charlie nods and moves to the driver's door, waving Orloski around to the passenger side.

The summer morning is cool, and under the canopy of the refueling area, the shade is enough to keep the cab of the Tahoe comfortable. Charlie looks around, and there are a few customers jockeying for positions at the pumps. He starts his vehicle and pulls to the far end of the lot, next to an idling semi truck hitched to a grain trailer. Charlie puts the Tahoe in park and adjusts the air conditioning as the engine idles. Out in the sun, the vehicle warms quickly, and he flips the fan to a higher setting. Charlie turns to his passenger and smiles. "Whadda ya know, Mr. Orloski, on this fine day?"

Charlie's phrasing of the question draws a smile from the stoic man. Orloski scratches the unkempt hair on his head, further mussing the splotch of thinning, brown and gray hair. Orloski is dressed in a cheap, charcoal-colored, suit. His presence is like that of a husky life insurance salesman, somewhat non-threatening, but at the same time not quite comfortable. His smile disappears as he speaks, "By now I'm sure you know my background."

Charlie nods, "And your buddy. Where is he today?"

"Never mind," Orloski frowns as he reaches into his interior jacket pocket, pulling out a letter. Charlie can see the letter is addressed to Father Franzen and, even with the small print, he can see the return address is Susan Montgomery.

"Hmmm," Charlie muses, not understanding the dramatics.

Orloski holds the letter. "Please, let me finish before you get too excited about what I say."

Orloski locks eyes with Charlie. Charlie begins to speak, "I...," he stops himself and nods to Orloski, who hands the letter to Charlie.

Orloski breaks eye contact and stares out to the highway at a passing car. "That letter," he begins, "I took it from the priest's cabin." He meets Charlie's eyes again. "I was staking out his cabin the last month, waiting for the word, per orders from my boss."

Charlie's eyes narrow, puzzled by the information. His head shakes, "What? Why?"

Orloski holds up a hand, "Let me finish. I was a ways down the road, just keepin' an eye on things. It was dark. I could barely hear the shot, but I could see the flash plain as day."

"Gunshot?" Charlie asks.

Orloski's head nods almost imperceptibly, "Yeah. I got out of my car and snuck to the cabin, carefully. Slowly. I was almost there when I heard and saw the second shot. It was pretty dark, but I saw somebody leave by boat. No motor. They musta rowed away or maybe a silent trolling motor."

"I don't understand," Charlie flinches. "Why were you there? Waiting for what word?" Charlie comprehends the coded words Orloski is using. He eases back in his seat. "You were waiting for word to kill Father Franzen." Charlie blinks rapidly as the words sink in.

"That letter," Orloski nods to the letter in Charlie's hand. "It might explain how somebody beat me to the punch. I know it was her. I'm positive."

"I don't...what...?" Charlie is at a loss for words. "You were going to kill the priest?" Charlie pinches the bridge of his nose. "I'm so confused." He looks to the man in the seat next to him. "You are telling an officer of the law you were going to kill a man?" Charlie points an accusing finger at Orloski.

Orloski holds his hand up in a "stop sign" fashion, "Nobody used those words." He heaves a heavy sigh, "Listen. It was no secret about Father Michael Franzen's, let's say, proclivities for boys." He rolls his eyes. "Let me correct myself. Everyone in the family was familiar with Father Franzen's problem, except save one naïve nephew, Gabe." Orloski throws his hands up in frustration. "Hell, if it was up to me, this would have been resolved three decades ago."

Charlie stares at the man in the passenger seat, not knowing how to react. Orloski continues, "Every family's got its secrets, but there was something very wrong with that priest." The man drags his hand over his mop of hair again in frustration. "What am I supposed to do?" Orloski holds his index finger and his thumb about an inch apart. "The boss, Gabe's dad, is about this far from having me put the boy down now, like you would with a mad dog." He balls up his fist and releases it, repeating the clenching action over and over as he speaks. "Gabe flipped out when he read the newspaper stories. They were favorite uncle, favorite nephew. Gabe is in total denial." Orloski throws his hands in the air in contempt. "He's dragging the whole family down, thinking he can un-tarnish Father Franzen's name...Lord knows that ship sailed a long, long time ago."

"So," Charlie finally responds, "why are you coming to me?"

"Gabe doesn't know I'm talking to you. Hell, he doesn't know anything. I'm sure you read his file. He did some time for his father's, shall I say error, and Gabe was given a pass. He does or does not do whatever he wants. His father lets him run wild." Orloski chews his tongue for a moment, "I didn't mean to say that. I think you know what I mean. Long story short, I am a fixer. I'm here to take care of this problem. That letter is evidence, strong evidence against that woman." He gathers his final thoughts. "Make the case against Ms. Montgomery, and Gabe can have closure. He'll get back to the Cities and out of your hair."

Charlie looks at the envelope. "What's in this letter?"

Orloski jabs a finger at the letter. "You can read it and interpret it, but it's pretty damning as far as I can tell. Susan Montgomery, former nun, seems pretty threatening toward the priest." Charlie nods and Orloski continues, "Gabe wants what he thinks is justice, i.e., Gabe putting a bullet into somebody's head. Shit. I'm bustin' my ass tryin' to get him back to the Cities, but you know how young kids are."

"Stubborn," Charlie clips the word.

"That's putting it mildly," Orloski sighs. "He won't let it go."

Charlie places the letter inside the console of his Tahoe and turns back to his passenger. "Father Franzen died of a heart attack. That's what the coroner's report concluded."

Orloski snorts a laugh, "I made the mistake of telling Gabe I thought I heard shots. I was nearby." Orloski grins weakly. "Somebody shot near him. Scared him to death. Is that murder? Somebody dies during the commission of a felony? Breaking and entering? Does that become murder?"

Charlie locks eyes with Orloski, the conversation is over. Charlie mulls over what he has just heard as Orloski exits the vehicle. Now he has a letter, stolen, obviously corrupted evidence, handed to him by a known gangster. Orloski points a finger at Susan based on circumstantial evidence. But, added to the ammo in the cooler the facts are compounding. Charlie decides it might be time to discuss some hypothetical situations with the FBI, but for now he'll wait. His eyes follow Orloski. The large man's head is on a swivel as he walks to his car, checking and rechecking his surroundings. Charlie shakes his head, wondering how a man can live such a life.

Chapter 32

Red Eyes

Near Hankinson, North Dakota

The Dakota Magic Casino and Hotel is a modest Las Vegas style casino rising out of the heavy, black soils of the Red River Valley. Nestled just inside the South Dakota border, it is the northernmost of the Sisseton-Wahpeton Tribe's gambling infrastructure. The 1980's brought the gambling compact between the State of South Dakota and the Tribe and soon thereafter, money was gifted to the state by the Tribe to build an interchange in the middle of the prairie on Interstate 29 in order to accommodate the casino. Geography and politics contributed to the odd location for the casino, but the treaties, gambling compacts, and reservation boundaries strangely and arbitrarily plunked the casino down in what everyone would consider a rural and remote location. Yet, the casino and hotel provide employment for tribal members and a place to play and stay for interstate highway travelers.

Tonight is a well deserved night away for Charlie and Veronica. Veronica is leaving the newspaper on its own for a day or two, and Charlie is trying to escape the conversation he had shared with Mr. Orloski earlier in the week. In the lobby, Charlie and Veronica check into their room at the front desk. Charlie notices the key cards he has been handed are stamped with the word "Suite." He is turning back to the front desk attendant when two smartly dressed, Native American men with jet-black, long, flowing hair commandeer Charlie's and Veronica's luggage. "Hey, what are you…" a cry from Charlie goes up and is cut off as he realizes who the men are. The men halt and turn around slowly. "Donald? Ronald?" Charlie questions.

Veronica stands in stunned silence, unable to do anything but raise a finger in confused protest and point at the men. The two brothers stand beside the cardboard cutouts of themselves that are part of the advertising for their headlining show that evening. Veronica's mouth is agape as she points a finger between the smiling men and the signage.

"Come on." Donald sweeps his hand forward. "Follow me."

Charlie grabs Veronica's hand and tows her along toward the bank of elevators. Donald and Ronald Red Eyes, Donald, the older brother, in the lead pushes the button for the elevator as the rest of the crew catches up. Donald sets his suitcase down as Charlie introduces Veronica and Ronald follows suit as they wait for the elevator. Charlie announces dramatically, "The headliners we came to see tonight. Sisseton's very own, Red Eyes! Donald and Ronald!"

The men bow deeply, reacting appropriately to Charlie's fabulous introduction. Veronica is hugged by each man and kissed on each cheek, drawing a comment from Charlie, "How very European of you. Don't forget, I am a police officer and carry a gun."

"Always the authority," Donald comments. Donald and Ronald could be twins. Donald, forty two years old and Ronald at forty years old, both look like they could pass for thirty. Movie star looks and charisma oozing from every pore, paired with tailored black slacks, white dress shirts, and hand-beaded leather vests set them apart from everyone else in the casino's hotel lobby. The similar clothes add that much more to the perception that the men are twins.

The elevator arrives and Ronald and Donald grab the luggage once again. Charlie shakes his head as they ride to the top floor. "You guys look like my kid brothers." He turns to Veronica. "These guys are my age," his voice goes high in disbelief.

"It's what clean living can do for you," Donald winks at Veronica.

Ronald follows up the statement, "Yeah, clean livin' and six months off every year!"

"Work hard, play hard," Donald laughs. "Or in our case vacation hard."

"Where do you guys live then," Veronica inquires, "when you're not touring?"

"We're in California, L.A." Ronald replies. "That's why we look this way, you got to blend in out there. A spa day keeps the doctor away!"

Out of the elevator and to the suite Charlie and Veronica follow the men carrying their suitcases. "You guys are next to us. Best rooms in the hotel. We upgraded you."

Charlie opens the door with his card key, and they move into the lavish room with large picture windows providing a bird's-eye view of the flat prairie and farmland below.

"Anything you need, it's on us," Donald moves forward and hugs Charlie tightly. Ronald moves close and hugs Charlie as soon as Donald lets him go.

Donald lets go of his hug, but holds onto Charlie's arms. "How are you, my friend?"

Charlie smiles and shakes his head, "Obviously not as good as you. You guys look fantastic. I can't wait to hear you play tonight."

Veronica, ever the reporter, questions Donald, "How do you know Charlie?"

Donald flashes a smile to Charlie before turning back to Veronica. "Charlie and I go way back to kindergarten. We knew each other all through school. He went with basketball and the army. Ron and I went with music."

Ronald steps forward. "That's half the story." He puts an arm around Charlie, "Charlie was our guardian angel. When I was in kindergarten and those guys were in first grade, well, let's just say Don and I were considered sissies."

Donald laughs, "That's probably putting it mildly. More like, prissy, sissy poofs."

Ronald smiles a closed lip smile of a clown. "People bullied us, and we got beat up a lot." Ronald squeezes his arm around Charlie, who smiles at the attention. "That is until Charlie stepped in and set everyone straight."

Donald laughs, "Once we were friends with Charlie, nobody bothered us anymore; in fact they wanted to be our friends too!"

"We owe this guy a lot," Ronald's emotions get the better of him a moment. "I'm not sure we'd be where we are, but for what Charlie did." He wipes at a watery eye. "Under Charlie's protection, I was able to be and become what I am today without fear."
Ronald hugs Charlie tightly. "Thank you, Charlie."

Charlie pats Ronald on the back as he looks to Veronica. "These guys exaggerate. You are welcome, Ronald. And thank you, for this beautiful suite. It's wonderful." Charlie sweeps his hand toward the ornate decorations and luxury furniture. "I'm so glad you can come slumming for a few days off your international tour."

"Slumming?" Donald shouts in rebuttal. "There's no place like home! Sweet home South Dakota!" Donald puts his hands on his hips. "Besides we are finished with our tour. This is our last couple gigs before we start vacation."

Ronald playfully pushes Charlie aside. "Hey, be nice. Don't talk about slummin'. This is our birthplace!" Ronald quickly has his arm back around Charlie's shoulder. "There's no better place to recharge the batteries. And we can give back to our hometown…and reservation. Plus, we can go get some of Mom's home cookin.'" Ronald's eyebrows bounce as he gives his brother a look.

"Yeah, right," Donald waves away Ronald's words. "Our trainer would kill us if we indulge in some of those fry bread, Indian tacos."

"My mouth just waters," Ronald says dreamily. "What Cameron, our trainer," Ronald huskily whispers the name toward Veronica, "doesn't know, won't hurt him."

Veronica smiles. "We'll never tell."

"So, you guys are doing three shows?"

"Yup," Donald pipes up. "Three nights of shows on the home turf, piece of cake to start a vacation."

"What I really wanna know is," Charlie looks back and forth between Ronald and Donald, "how did you convince the Sax Pack to open for you?"

Donald shrugs, "They owed us a favor…"

"And," Ronald cuts off his brother, "a couple of those guys got roots and family in the Twin Cities." Charlie nods in appreciation of the answer to his question. "Why don't you get settled, then maybe come on down to the theatre to see our rehearsal. Donald and I are writing some new stuff. Maybe you want to sit in?"

"That would be fantastic!" Veronica shouts almost before Ronald is done speaking.

The brothers move to the door. "And," Donald points a finger at Charlie, "you will be joining us for dinner after the show. Our wives will be there. They are dying to see you."

Charlie nods, "You bet. We'll be there."

"See you in a bit," Ronald waves as he departs, pulling the door closed behind them.

Veronica jumps into Charlie's arms. "This is so awesome, but did he say wives?"

Charlie laughs, "Yes, they are married. I know they seem a bit effeminate, but, you know, California and all."

Veronica laughs as she kisses Charlie's cheek. "Thank you so much. Why didn't you tell me about all this?"

"I wanted to surprise you," Charlie shrugs.

"Well," Veronica shakes her head, "I am truly surprised." She holds a finger to a lip. "Hey, do you think they would do an interview for the paper?"

"I don't see why not," Charlie nods.

Veronica kisses Charlie. "Oh, this is so great!"

Chapter 33

Leaves of Fall

It is a full house for a night of "Smooth Jazz on the Prairie" as the marquee sign at the front of the casino indicates. Charlie and Veronica enjoy front row seats as the entertainers perform. The Sax Pack, made up of saxophonists, as the name might indicate, opens for the duo of brothers, Red Eyes. It is not often that smooth jazz graces the rural Dakotas, and the capacity crowd is particularly moved by the funky, uplifting tunes of the Sax Pack. The Sax Pack is a group of sax players, Jeff Kashiwa, Steve Cole, and Marcus Anderson. Each a star in his own right, they have banded together to put out some music and form a powerhouse touring group. When you hear their music, it is impossible not to smile and tap your toe. It is Jeff Kashiwa who finishes the opening act's set with one of his biggest hits "Hyde Park (The Ah, Oooh Song)" that gets complete audience participation and finally sets the stage for Red Eyes. "It's time," Jeff announces through the microphone on the stage. "The ones you've been waiting for, Red Eyes!"

With a flash of lights like lightning and the sound effect of thunder, Ronald and Donald take the stage. Donald on trumpet and Ronald on keyboards are a treat for the audience. They are joined by the backup band, The Hedge of Night, consisting of bass, guitar, drums, and percussion. Their opening tune is "Native Thunder," the medium tempo hit that builds into their most commercial hit, "Peony" that is featured in a TV commercial for Cadillac. The playlist always includes Donald's medley of songs in tribute to a mentor, Herb Alpert. Ronald gets the spotlight a moment with his comedic stylings that include organ music that one would hear at a baseball game; "Take Me Out to the Ballgame" rings in the rafters. The musicians get a chance to catch their breath for a moment before Ronald hands the crowd's attention back to Donald.

It is Donald who takes the lead in introducing the band. Ronald plays his keyboards, providing an almost reverential, Sunday hymn underneath the introductions. "I'd like to introduce the band," Donald announces, the crowd cheers politely. "Our band is known as the 'Hedge of Knight;' of course, this is a nod to the world of TV soap operas." The crowd manages a ripple of laughter. Ronald finishes introducing each band member. The cascading chimes emanate from the percussion section, and the crowd roars its approval, hearing the first notes of a favorite song. Donald encourages the crowd by waving his arms; trumpet in hand as he continues, "The 'Hedge of Knight' band is our special homage to the soap opera world, the theme to the afternoon drama, "Roses in the Clouds."

Ronald tinkles his keyboard producing the familiar chords. Donald looks to Ronald. "This song, it paid for our houses in Beverly Hills?"

Ronald smiles and nods as he plays, finally answering, "And then some."

Donald positions his trumpet to play, but moves it down and steps back to the microphone. "This song is dedicated to our mom. She's under the weather tonight, but she told me she's coming out to see us tomorrow."

The crowd cheers, and the extended introduction plays on with the guitar and bass joining Ronald's keyboard. "Ronald and I wrote this song, and I can proudly tell you that Herb Alpert himself told me that he wished he had written this tune."

The crowd applauds with a mixture of laughter and cat calls as the introduction builds. "Ladies and gentleman," Donald points to Ronald, picking up the beat with snaps of his fingers, "my favorite song, and I hope it's yours too, 'Leaves of Fall.'"

Donald plays the romantic, haunting, mid-tempo ballad. The song finishes with a roar of the crowd. Donald bows and throws his hands in the direction of his brother, who also takes a bow. "Whew, let me catch my breath," Donald gasps a bit. "That song's getting tougher for me in my old age." Donald wipes down with a towel. "We just have a couple more songs, and we'll be wrapping up, but we got a special treat for you. The Sax Pack is back!" The opening act files on the stage, saxophones in hand to the roar of the crowd. Donald continues, "We have a new tune out, you may have heard it on the adult contemporary chart. It's called 'Power' and with the help of the boys from Sax Pack, we're going to play it." The bass drum thumps loudly and backs off into a steady rhythm from the high-hat cymbal. "It's nice to be home on the reservation, and I'd like to recognize my special guest tonight." Donald points to Charlie in the front row as the keyboards begin to establish a rhythmic string of chords. "Many of you know him; he is a life long friend of Ronald and me, Charlie LeBeau! Charlie, please stand." Charlie reluctantly half stands and waves to the crowd. "This song is for you, Charlie!" The crowd applauds, but a smattering of boos rain down. "Whoa! Sounds like we have a few members of the crowd that have had a run in with the law!" Donald laughs. "Thank you, Charlie!"

The song lives up to its name. With Donald at the lead with his trumpet and the Sax Pack's three saxophones wailing, the almost rocking song is a funky beat to dance and move to.

*   *   *   *

The concert is over and Donald, Ronald, and the musicians from the band are joined by Charlie and Veronica in the restaurant. Seven Fires Grill, the casino restaurant, is closed for the night except for its special guests. Members of the party eat, drink, talk, and laugh. The adrenaline from the performance slowly wears off. Donald shares a couple of stories of his misadventures with Charlie as kids, including the horrible prank they played on their mothers involving an overnight campout in a tent in the backyard. Donald tells the story of nearly giving his mother a heart attack with a bucket of red paint splattered on the tent, and an old rusty knife left strategically at the scene. "They called the police for that one," Donald shakes his head. "A toast." Donald raises his glass of wine. "To friends." Everyone raises a glass and repeats, "To friends."

The evening runs into early morning. Charlie and Veronica excuse themselves.

"Thanks for the lovely evening," Veronica provides a tired wave.

"Have a good night," Charlie gives a salute to everyone at the table. "Maybe we'll see you at breakfast tomorrow."

*   *   *   *

Charlie and Veronica move arm and arm away from the restaurant. They cross the lobby and make their way toward the elevators. Gabe Franzen sits in wait where the casino begins in the first row of slot machines. A drunken verbal ambush from Gabe begins as Gabe shoots from his seat at a slot machine. Charlie and Veronica are almost to the elevators when he stumbles and yells across the polished tile of the lobby, "Worthless cop! My uncle's murdered, and you're doin' nothin'!"

Gabe strings together slurred profanities as he approaches Charlie, who moves Veronica behind him to shield her. Gabe is fairly intimidating in his black jeans and his billowing, black leather trench coat even in the summer heat.

Charlie is ready to end the night, and he would prefer not to have to deal with an inebriated, sweating, punk kid. "Stay behind me," he whispers to Veronica.

Veronica is frightened. She tucks herself tightly behind her man. "Be careful, Charlie," she whispers.

A sleepy Vincent Orloski, pushing buttons on his slot machine finally realizes what the commotion is in the lobby. His job of keeping an eye on Gabe took a momentary backseat to weariness and the hypnotic spinning of the slot machine's wheels. The burly man is a blur, surprisingly light on his feet for his heft; he sprints toward Charlie and Gabe. Orloski is late arriving, but he is there in time to use a basketball box out move, placing his body between Charlie and Gabe. "Sorry, LeBeau. I got 'im."

Charlie and Veronica keep an eye over their shoulders as they make their way to the elevators. Charlie presses the button, the doors open, and they move inside. Orloski restrains Gabe amidst the fuming man's diatribe-filled profanity. The cursing finally ends with the closing of the elevator doors.

Gabe muscles free from Orloski, who eases away. In a flash Gabe peels back to Orloski, grabbing his partner in crime by the lapels of his jacket. He hisses through gritted teeth, "I could kill you."

Casino security slowly encircles the men, filtering in slowly from every direction. Gabe sees the guards and shoves Orloski to the floor. Security moves forward. "It's all right! I'm fine! Nothing to see here!" he shouts as he springs back to his feet. Orloski holds up his hands, trying to keep security at bay. "It's ok. We're going outside. No worries."

Orloski herds Gabe outside through the sliding doors of the entrance and out into the cool, clammy air of the summer night.

Chapter 34

Wants vs. Needs

Outside the front entrance of the Dakota Magic Casino it is as nearly bright as day. The security lights, the marquee lights, and the ever changing billboard lights illuminate the front of the casino. Gabe leans against a light pole smoking a cigarette. Fifty yards away, at the opposite side of the entrance, Orloski does the same. The men stare at each other across the distance. A few straggling gamblers move out of the casino, interrupting the long distance stare down. A half hour passes and multiple cigarettes litter the concrete at each man's feet. Gabe walks a few feet away to stretch his legs. Orloski closes the distance, moving to the side of Gabe's newly adjusted position, leaning against the rail surrounding a concrete planter holding shrubs and flowers in the middle of the sidewalk heading to the entrance. The plants drip with water having just been the subject of a shower from the automated irrigation system. Orloski leans on the rail just a few feet from his counterpart. "What do you want?" Gabe growls. He speaks in a mumble, without removing the cigarette from his lips.

"Are you calmed down?" Orloski asks. The men do not look at each other. Each man stares ahead at the ever-changing Las Vegas-style billboard in front of them.

"What do you want?" Gabe repeats his question.

"I want to go home," Orloski flatly replies.

"Go then," Gabe orders, his voice rising to almost a shout.

Orloski's head shakes, his lips purse before he finally answers calmly, "You gotta let this go, Kid. You know I can't go home 'til you go home. Those are your father's orders. Where you go, I go."

Gabe's eyes momentarily glance to the big man lecturing him. "He's getting to be an old man."

"But, he's still the boss," Orloski sighs. "Wants versus needs. Isn't that what your dad says? Think about what your dad's taught you all these years. Look at your father, he's willing to let this whole thing go, and it was his brother." He slowly waves an arm as if shooing a fly away. "Just let it fade away."

Gabe frowns, "He won't be boss forever."

The men do not look at each other. They stare straight ahead. The video billboard signs animated messages bathe their faces in constantly varying hues and intensities of color, providing a surreal effect to the conversation. "This thing with your uncle; it's a loser. You got to let it go."

Gabe's drunken emotions get the better of him. His lip quivers and his eyes well with tears. He drops his head and stares at the ground. "He was my uncle," his voice cracks.

Orloski reaches out a hand, but hesitates. "It's like you said, nothing lasts forever." He extends his hand and places it on Gabe's shoulder. He squeezes down, trying to push the tension out of the suffering man. "Your uncle was seventy-five years old. That's a good, long life. This is not a tragedy."

Gabe straightens, gathering himself. He doesn't look at the man at his side. He shrugs away the comforting hand on his shoulder. Speaking slowly and firmly, Gabe does not make eye contact, "Vince, this is the last time I'm going to say this. Stay out of my way."

Orloski watches in silence as Gabe pushes away from the railing and walks briskly toward the parking lot.

Chapter 35

Yellow Jacket

LeBeau Residence

Nat sits at the kitchen table. Piles of letters and papers surround him. He reads the outside of the envelope, noting it is from Winona State University in Minnesota. He slices through the envelope and reads the form letter. At the bottom of the page is a hand-written note that states, "I'd like to come visit you and discuss your future! Cheers, Coach Mickelson."

This letter goes into the pile Nat has categorized as "maybe." The biggest pile in front of Nat is the "no chance" stack.

Claude approaches the kitchen table. "Holy cow, Nat. You better not let Charlie see your mess on this table. You know how he is with his militaristic feelings on a clean kitchen table."

"Don't worry, Grandpa," Nat replies with a laugh. "I'll have things sorted out before he gets home."

"The letters never stop coming, do they?" Claude takes a seat at the table and picks up the letter from Winona State University. "Hey, this one has a note from the coach."

"Yeah, it's in the 'maybe' pile," Nat nods as he picks up another envelope, this one sporting a large, red "N" indicating the University of Nebraska.

Claude picks up an unopened envelope. "Here's one from Northern."

Nat shakes his head and frowns, "Nope, not going there." Nat knows his grandfather favors Northern and is disappointed by this decision.

"Why?" Claude questions, hurt by the out-and-out rejection. "Northern is close. We could see you play all the time."

Nat shakes his head, "They run a 'slow it down' offense. I wanna get out and run." Nat looks at his grandfather's pained look at the quick dismissal. "I'll tell you what, if I get no other offers, I'll go to Northern, even if I have to try to walk on."

Claude smiles, satisfied with the response. He nods to the letter in Nat's hand, "How about Nebraska? Big Ten? Cornhusker, eh?"

Nat shakes his head, "Nah. I'd have to redshirt, then I'd be on the bench, probably the first two years. I wanna play now. I'm not gettin' any younger."

Claude laughs, "You don't know anything about gettin' old."

A knock on the door interrupts the discussion. Nat pushes himself up from his chair and ambles to the front door. Opening the door he finds a young, white man dressed in blue jeans and a shiny, dark green sweat-suit jacket. Emblazoned on the chest of the jacket is an embroidered image resembling a wasp. "Hi. Are you Nat?" the man asks. "My name is Coach Vitter, Oscar Vitter. Black Hills State University Head Basketball Coach." The forty year old man extends his hand, and Nat looks at him a moment before grasping and shaking his hand. Nat looks to his grandfather, who signals with a wave of his hand to let the man in.

"You want to come in?" Nat questions.

"Sure," Coach Vitter smiles a big smile as Nat steps aside, allowing the coach to enter. Claude stands and clicks the radio off, halting Vance Joy and his song "Riptide" mid-warble. The coach is about the same size as Nat and moves with the grace of an athlete across the living room to the kitchen, introducing himself to Claude. "Coach Oscar Vitter," he says with the polished ease of many introductions on the recruiting trail.

"Nice to meet you," Claude shakes his hand. "I'm Claude LeBeau, Nat's grandpa."

Oscar Vitter is a former college basketball player and, with his baby-face and slicked back hair, he could probably still pass for one, but now he's the third year coach of the men's basketball team at Black Hills State University. "I brought some baseball caps for you, if you like," Coach Vitter holds up a dark green cap and a white cap, both with the hornet emblem.

"Awesome," Nat says as he grabs the hats and examines them. "Is it a bee? A wasp?" he questions as he looks to the coach.

Coach Vitter laughs, "I see you haven't looked much at Black Hills State. It's a yellow-jacket. That's our mascot."

"Oh, sorry," Nat nods. "It's cool."

"Would you like a glass of water?" Claude offers.

"Sure," Coach Vitter nods.

Claude waves to the kitchen table, "Have a seat." Claude grabs a glass and fills it with water as the coach moves to the table.

"Holy cow!" Coach Vitter exclaims as he sees the piles of recruiting letters on the table. "Am I too late?" he glances back and forth between Claude and Nat, a big smile beams from his face. "I hope you haven't made a decision. I am here to offer you a full basketball scholarship, today."

"Really?" Nat questions.

Claude points at a chair as he sits. "You drive all the way over here for this?"

The coach sits and Nat follows suit. "I'm on my way back from a basketball camp in Minneapolis. I was in the area and thought I'd just drop by." The coach turns his attention to Nat. "I'd think you'd fit it great with our program. If you can play point guard, and from the videos I've seen, you can, you could start right away. Our point guard is going to graduate, and you could step right in. I want to stress that he's going to graduate." The coach holds up three fingers. "In my three years, every four year player has graduated, and every player is on track to graduate. I emphasize education. We want to win, but a college education is the most important thing." The coach readjusts in his chair. "I tell all my recruits this up front, if you come to Black Hills State to play, it's unlikely that you have a pro basketball career in your future. Thus, we focus on academics."

Claude nods in agreement at the coach's statement. Nat doesn't say anything. He nods as he looks back and forth between Claude and the coach. "Let me ask you something, Nat," Coach Vitter looks intently at the young man across the table from him. "What are you looking to study? A lot of our players follow an education major with a minor in coaching, but we got a lot of choices at Black Hills State."

The coach struggles to read Nat's expression. Nat works hard to contain his excitement, he doesn't even smile; it is all business, "I'm looking at journalism, but teaching is on my list. My mom was a teacher."

"I heard about your mom, my condolences."

"Thank you," Nat nods.

Coach Vitter scoots up in his chair as he leans forward toward Nat. "Listen, we got a great English Department. You can get a good writing background in class and hands on experience with the school newspaper, the 'Jacket Journal.' Plus, I probably don't need to tell you, it's the beautiful Black Hills, where the climate is a far cry from the rest of South Dakota." Coach Vitter grins.

Nat grins. He looks to his grandfather who shrugs. The coach is back into full recruiting mode, waving his hand over the piles of letters on the table. "I can see my competition is blanketing you with paper."

Claude chimes in, "I just opened one from the University of Nebraska."

Coach Vitter nods, "Nice, but I'm betting they didn't offer a scholarship in their letter. I'm not here to beat around the bush; I'm here to offer Nat a scholarship, a full scholarship." Coach Vitter turns to Nat. "What do you say, Nat? You want to be a Yellow Jacket?" He reaches into his pocket and pulls out a cell phone. "One phone call and I can have the early commitment papers here in a few minutes. No muss, no fuss, no more hassles from other coaches. What do you think?"

Nat grimaces, "I can't say yes...yet. I gotta talk to my uncle."

Coach Vitter nods and smiles painfully at the rejection. He pushes his hands off his knees and stands. He draws a business card out of his wallet. "Here's my card; call me anytime. If you have a question, I'll get you an answer. My cell phone number is on there. Twenty-four-seven, give me a call. We'd love to have you at Black Hills State."

Nat and Claude stand as Coach Vitter extends a hand shaking Nat's hand first, then Claude's. "I apologize for the unannounced intrusion, but I just had to meet Nat in person. I've seen plenty of video, and, again, I think you'd fit in nicely as a Yellow Jacket."

The coach moves to the door and Nat opens it, letting the man out onto the porch. "Thanks for your time. Have a great day." With an easy wave the man jogs smoothly down the stairs and to his car.

Nat holds up the business card. "I'll let you know."

Chapter 36

Play For It

Charlie LeBeau's Driveway

The end of Charlie's nine to five shift finds him pulling his Tahoe into his driveway, but he is waved back by Nat who is dribbling and shooting baskets on the driveway, which is a combination concrete slab, gravel, and sun-baked dirt. Charlie parks the vehicle giving plenty of room for Nat's practice. He heads for the house with Nat calling after him, "You ready?"

Charlie knows he's being challenged, but plays the part. "For what?" he answers holding his arms out inquisitively.

"To be schooled," Nat responds matter-of-factly.

Charlie laughs. "Let me change my shoes," he calls out as he opens the door and moves in the house.

Nat flips a thumb's up toward his uncle and spins to the basket, launching a shot that rattles in. Nat notes the partial shade provided by the large cottonwood next to the driveway. The sun in the late afternoon sky filters through the leaves onto the court and backboard, providing an added degree of difficulty to each shot. The leaves of the tree rustle in the slight breeze, also providing another factor influencing each shot. Nat continues to shoot from everywhere on the court.

* * * *

Inside the house, Claude notes Charlie's arrival with a shout, "You're home! Did Nat talk to ya?"

Charlie drops his utility belt on the couch and takes a seat next to it. He works on the laces of his boots. "He's waiting for me. I gotta at least change clothes."

Claude smiles, "He got an offer today. Full scholarship to Black Hills State."

Charlie pauses the task of unlacing his boots. "What?" He stares at his dad.

Claude moves from the kitchen to the living room as he explains, "The head coach, Coach Vitter, was passing through on his way back from Minneapolis. He came in, had a glass of water, and matter-of-factly made the offer, and went on his merry way. Five minutes, tops."

Charlie works on his boot laces again and kicks a boot off his foot. "Did he take it?"

Claude laughs, "It all happened so fast." He shakes his head, "The boy told the coach he had to talk to you."

Charlie laughs, "I see." Charlie shakes his head and chuckles. He nods to the driveway outside. "He's gonna play me for it."

*   *   *   *

Charlie exits the house and moves down the porch stairs. When his foot hits the ground Nat tosses the ball to him. Charlie takes a dribble on the sidewalk and launches a shot from about thirty feet. He holds a picture perfect follow through as he stares at the rim, waiting for the high, arcing shot to hit its mark. It does. It is a swish. "Woo-boy! I'm feelin' it tonight!" Charlie hollers. It's a side of this personality that is hidden, except while competing on the basketball court. Charlie is confident and boisterous about his ability when he is playing the game he loves, especially with his nephew. The competition between the two tends to heat up quickly, and tonight was no different.

Nat collects the ball and tosses it to his uncle on the move, edging toward the basket. Charlie catches and shoots from about twenty feet and again it is a swish. Charlie cocks his head as he looks at his nephew, "You sure you want to try me tonight?"

Charlie pokes at the ball as Nat dribbles. He backs off and drains a sixteen foot jumper. "The Black Hills State coach came by today. He made me an offer. Full scholarship."

Charlie shoots a short bank shot that drops in. He rebounds the ball and tosses it to Nat. "That's what Claude was saying when I was inside."

Nat clanks a bank shot, and Charlie rebounds the ball and maneuvers for a reverse layup. "Black Hills State, huh?" Charlie questions.

Charlie grabs the ball and dribbles between his legs. He looks at his nephew, who just shrugs. "I told him I needed to talk to you."

"What's your gut tell ya?" Charlie asks as he continues to dribble.

Nat's shoulders half shrug, snagging near his ears. "It's got everything I'm looking for. It's beautiful out there, that's for sure. It's got a teaching major, and he said I could major in English if I wanted to be a journalist."

"They got a school newspaper you could write for?"

"Jacket Journal, that's the name of it," Nat nods. "It's mostly on-line, but they still publish some paper copies periodically."

"Let's go then," Charlie flips the ball to Nat, "you take it first. You beat me, you call him tomorrow and tell him you commit. I win, you call him an' tell him you're still lookin'."

"Sounds good," Nat grabs the ball and tosses it back to Charlie as he moves across the driveway to the top of the hand-painted key marked on the makeshift court, "Check it."

Charlie checks the ball back to Nat and before Charlie can move up to defend, Nat rises and fires, knocking down the shot. "One zip," Nat announces trying to remain expressionless, but unable to contain a hint of a smile.

"Yikes, I wasn't ready." Charlie shakes his head.

"Well, Nat shrugs, "you shouldn't a checked the ball. Ball in." Nat and Charlie switch positions at the top of the key. Nat bounces the ball to his uncle. Charlie fakes a shot and crosses over on his dribble for a lay up. "You think they play defense out there in the Black Hills?" Charlie laughs unapologetically.

Nat shakes his head, "You're still pretty quick, Uncle Charlie. I never get used to an old guy moving so fast."

Charlie checks the ball back to Nat at the top of the key. He dribbles casually to the left then explodes past his uncle laying the ball over the rim. The ball goes back to Charlie who executes a spinning dribble past a gambling defensive play on Nat's part. It is a back and forth battle with constant conversation and trash talk. The older, stronger Charlie holds his own against the quicker, agile youngster. At a score of twelve to eleven in Nat's favor, the conversation turns back to the scholarship offer.

Charlie huffs and puffs, hands on his hips, "Looks like you want this." He checks the ball to Nat, holding his hand in front of his opponent's face, blocking his view. Charlie bends his knees, ready to move. Nat takes one dribble to the right and springs effortlessly in the air. He launches a fifteen foot jump shot from the elbow of the free-throw line. "Nothin' but net!" Nat gathers the ball. "Whew! It'd be nice to get it over with. Commit early and not have to deal with all the phone calls and letters."

Charlie is winded as he moves to the top of the key, hands on his hips. "Fine. Play to fifteen. Win by two. What's the score?"

Nat holds the ball with one hand, pressing it against his hip, ready to check to his uncle. He points to himself, "Thirteen to eleven, me."

Nat checks the ball to his uncle. Charlie dribbles left then to the right. He turns and backs the ball down the lane toward the basket, using his strength over Nat. Faking to the left he turns back to shoot a six foot fade away. Nat's length is too much for Charlie; he tips the shot to himself and dribbles to the top of the key. "Woo-hoo!" Nat exclaims backing away from the free throw line while facing the basket. He picks up his dribble and shoots an uncontested eighteen footer that swishes. Charlie throws his hands up in surrender. "One more, old man," Nat sneers. "Fourteen to eleven."

Charlie gathers the ball while executing a dramatic eye roll. He tosses the basketball to Nat and sets his feet at the top of the key. Nat checks the ball without a word. "Give it to me?" Charlie questions.

Nat backs off the defense, giving Charlie a wide open shot. Charlie launches from the top of the key. The ball is halfway down, but it spins out, and Nat rebounds it with authority. "Game point," Nat announces as he pounds the ball, dribbling the ball between his legs. He glides to the top of the key, maneuvering straight on to the basket. Charlie bends his knees and tightens up his defense. Nat sees Charlie lower as he bends his knees; Nat takes advantage popping a jumper from the top of the key. Swish.

Charlie collects the ball and palms it. Nat beams with pride. "Looks like we're done here."

"You got me," Charlie manages between breaths.

On cue, Claude is out of the house, standing on the porch. "What's for supper?" he yells.

"I don't know. What's a yellow jacket like to eat?" Charlie extends an elbow into the ribs of Nat, who flinches back.

Charlie shoves the ball into Nat's belly. "What?" a confused Claude calls out from his perch.

"Let's call in for pizza!" Charlie yells to Claude. "First, Nat's got to make twenty free-throws in a row. Get on the line. I'll rebound."

"I'm getting' hungry!" Claude calls out.

"Call it in. We'll go get it," Charlie responds, gathering the ball as Nat sinks his first free-throw. Claude is not moving. "Here, you come rebound, Dad," Charlie moves toward the house, "I'll go call it in."

Charlie and Claude trade positions.

*   *   *   *

Inside the house, Charlie grabs his cell phone and looks out the window at Claude rebounding the ball as Nat sinks another free throw. Charlie moves into Claude's bedroom. The room is neatly kept. A queen-sized bed takes up most of the space. A night stand and dresser are the only furniture. Charlie moves to the closet and opens the folding doors. He reaches up and grabs a cigar box. Charlie can feel the box is nearly empty, and he opens it to find only a couple stray .45 caliber cartridges rolling around inside next to a spare clip. "Hmm," Charlie grunts. "Where is the pistol?" he whispers aloud. He returns the box to the shelf, exits the room, and punches the button on his phone to dial the Hot Stuff Pizza store.

Chapter 37

A Promise Made, a Promise Kept

Sisseton, South Dakota

The television blares loudly in Room 211 at the Super 8 Motel. The gentle knock and soft call, "Sir" by the night desk clerk are overpowered by the TV's volume.

Gabe is sprawled on his bed half passed out, staring at the ceiling. His stupor is a result of a full night's drinking, first at the bowling alley, then at the American Legion. Finally, with Vincent Orloski's assistance, Gabe made it to his room, left with a bottle of vodka to put himself to bed.

"Sir, it's three o'clock in the morning. If you could just lower the TV volume; our other guests would like to sleep." The minimum wage worker knocks again.

A stone cold sober Orloski emerges from his room across the hall a couple doors down, dressed in a t-shirt, slacks, and oxford shoes. He appears the picture of a man who has hastily re-dressed, just out of bed for a quick appearance in public. He smiles a weak smile at the clerk. "I thought my night of babysitting was over." He points to the door handle. "Do you have a key card? He's my business partner. If you can let me in, I'll get it quieted down for the night."

The clerk uses a master card key to activate the mechanism, and Orloski pushes the door open. The dead bolt is not engaged, and he moves into the room, turning to the clerk. "I'll take it from here."

The clerk nods silently and moves down the hall. Orloski moves across the room, finds the TV remote, and mutes the TV. The dark room, illuminated only by the TV's flickering picture, casts twitching shadows on the wall. "Get some sleep," Orloski commands. "You have had a busy night, and there are other people here trying to sleep."

Gabe stares helplessly at the ceiling, seemingly oblivious to Orloski. Orloski taps Gabe's foot. "Get some sleep. I'll see you in the morning."

Orloski is not prepared for what happens next. Gabe is on his feet, blocking the path to the door, swinging a balled up fist, and landing a punch to Orloski's gut. Orloski doubles over, and Gabe drops him with a left handed punch to his cheek. Gabe stands over the unconscious Orloski. "Don't tell me what to do, old man."

It takes all of Gabe's strength to haul Orloski's hulking mass to his Lexus and load him into the passenger side. In the business that Gabe and Orloski are in, zip-tie restraints are common, and reaching into the glove box, Gabe pulls the plastic ties out and secures Orloski's hands and feet. A few strips of duct tape between the feet and the wrists, form a truss that locks down Orloski in his seat. Gabe straps the seatbelt around Orloski, shuts the passenger door, and looks around to see if anyone is watching. With nobody around, Gabe slips behind the wheel and points the car west, heading up South Dakota Highway 10.

Fifteen minutes later, Gabe spots the Sica Hollow State Park sign reflected in the darkness of the empty highway. He slows and turns his Lexus north onto Bureau of Indian Affairs Route 10. The jostling of the turn awakens Orloski. "Uhh," he groans in the passenger seat. He looks down at his restrained hands and feet, finally gathering enough wits, he looks to Gabe next to him. "What are you doing, Gabe? Come on, man, let me go."

Gabe doesn't answer, staring at the sliver of the road in front of him, illuminated by the powerful headlights. "Come on, let's just head back to Minneapolis," Orloski pleads. "You gotta let this go."

"Shut up!" Gabe explodes, "Shut your fucking mouth!" He does not look at his passenger as he continues to scream. "All I hear from you, 'Come on, Gabe, let it go.' I'm sick of it. I'm in charge here. I'll handle this!"

"What's your dad gonna say?" Orloski poses the question. "Not even your dad is interested in his own brother's death. You need to snap back to..."

The words are cut short as they exit Orloski's mouth. A left-hand jab from Gabe connects to left eye of Orloski, and he is out again. "Keep your mouth shut!" Gabe screams at the unconscious man.

The car winds down the gravel road, following the curves as it travels the hills of the Coteau des Prairie. They pass the sign directing travelers to Sica Hollow State Park, a sacred site of the Indians in the area. The hardwood covered hillsides of that coulee drain the top of the Coteau, a beautiful landscape, and one of the reasons the state of South Dakota set the area aside as a state park.

Gabe steers his Lexus past potholes, ponds, and the prairie grass of pastures separated from the road by sagging barbed wire fences. He's been down this road before, and he remembered one outstanding characteristic. About three miles south of Veblen he knows there is a large 10 foot by 12 foot concrete box culvert under the road. He made a mental note of it on his previous trip. This is as good of a place to take care of business as he can imagine. With the lights of Veblen illuminating the sky to the north, Gabe slows. The reflection of a black and yellow diagonally-lined sign indicating a culvert, shines back from his high intensity headlights. He pulls the vehicle to the shoulder of the road carefully, feeling for any softness. The last thing he wants now is to get stuck.

He finds the culvert he is looking for. The shoulder slopes down sharply at a five feet horizontal to a one foot vertical drop. Gabe is out of the car, dimming his headlights, and flipping the switch to parking lights only. He moves around to the passenger side and opens the door. He reaches in his pocket and extracts a knife. He flicks it open and slices the zip-tie restraint binding Orloski's feet, as well as the duct tape truss. He pockets the knife and slaps his passenger, trying to bring some life back into the man. Orloski groans groggily, and Gabe unfastens the seatbelt as he pulls on Orloski's bound arms. Free from the vehicle, Orloski is lead down the slope, stumbling, being pulled maliciously by Gabe. The parking lights of the Lexus provide just enough illumination to outline the mouth of the culvert. The men are about fifteen feet below the grade of the road when the vehicle's lights lose their effectiveness. Gabe pulls his cell phone from his pocket, and the screen acts as a makeshift flashlight. Orloski manages his final word as he is shoved into the spacious box culvert. "Why?" echoes through the culvert, hauntingly. Orloski does not have all of his faculties after the brutal punches. He is probably fortunate that he doesn't fully understand his fate. In the middle of the culvert, Gabe pushes Orloski to his knees. From the small of his back, Gabe reaches for the 9 millimeter Berretta. Without hesitation, he places two bullets in the back of Orloski's skull. Gabe shines his makeshift flashlight on the body beneath him. He dances slightly to avoid the blood rushing toward his feet on the down stream side of the culvert. He turns away from his partner of the last ten years and marches toward the opening of the culvert. His ears ring from the echoing roar of the gunshots. He can barely hear the thud of his steps reverberating on the concrete floor of the culvert. Out of the mouth of the culvert, Gabe stumbles over the rip-rap boulders that provide erosion protection from the rushing water when it rains. The ringing in his ears is amplified by the buzz of alcohol in his brain, and he struggles to return to his vehicle. He scrambles up the slope back to his running Lexus. He realizes he still has the pistol in his hand and checks the safety and stows the pistol in its holster at the small of his back. A promise made, a promise kept. Gabe had told Orloski he could kill him, and now Gabe has completed his vow.

Gabe gets back in his car still unsure of himself. The alcohol is still keeping everything fuzzy. From the hotel to the car, the drive, then to the culvert, Gabe felt like he was in a dream state. Everything is becoming real. He can see the lights of Veblen ahead. He puts the car in gear and slams the accelerator to the floor. The front wheel drive Lexus spews gravel from its tires, lurching forward, north toward the lights.

In Veblen, Gabe turns east onto South Dakota Highway 25. He obeys the speed limit and makes his way to Claire City and New Effington, back to Interstate 29. Then south back to Sisseton, Gabe tries to reconcile the night's events. Back to the Super 8 and his motel room, he falls on his bed as the sun starts to rise.

Chapter 38

Oh, Deer

Sisseton, South Dakota

The morning and afternoon come and go. Gabe is still passed out on his motel bed. He finally awakes to the orange sunset forming a glowing halo around his curtains. His temples pound from the hangover. He squeezes his head between his hands and makes his way to the bathroom. He notices he is still fully clothed as he relieves himself. He washes his hands, staring at the scruffy face in the mirror. Squinting he recognizes a greenish-yellow tint to his complexion. His mind is foggy. He returns to the edge of his bed and sits, again jamming his hands against his head a moment before returning to the bathroom. He rummages through his shaving kit and with a shaky hand finds a bottle of Tylenol. He takes the maximum dose with a scoop of water from his hand to aid in swallowing.

The reality hits him, and he whispers aloud, "Vincent." He opens his door a crack and looks down the empty hallway. The "Do Not Disturb" sign falls from the door handle to the floor. He moves into the corridor and sidles in front of Room 208 and taps on the door. "Vincent," he calls out softly. His mind knows it's a lost cause, but he is reluctant to accept the truth.

Back in his room, Gabe sits in the motel chair, an uncomfortable, mostly decorative piece of furniture. He slouches in place for a half hour, racking his brain over the previous night's events. Startling himself, he leaps to his feet, donning his leather jacket. He feels the key to his Lexus in his pocket and moves from his room, heading to the motel parking lot.

*   *   *   *

It is dusk, and the parking lot lights hum overhead. Gabe is in his car now, pulling out of the lot and heading west once again on South Dakota Highway 10. Less than 24 hours ago he drove the same route in darkness then, and now he repeats his path. Up the Coteau, past the golf course, he winds his way on Highway 10 until he sees the brown sign reflected by his lights indicating Sica Hollow State Park. The Lexus carries Gabe north. In the distance he can see the lights of Veblen. He crosses over the culvert where the body of his friend lies. His eyes welling with tears, the remote possibility of this being just a bad dream evaporates. He steps on the accelerator and heads toward Veblen. Gravel churns under the tires, clinking and clunking off the car's undercarriage. In a few minutes, Gabe is in Veblen, cruising east on South Dakota Highway 25, just as he had the night before. He sees the clock on his dashboard change from 9:59 to 10:00 before his eyes. He lays his foot down harder on the accelerator; up ahead a vehicle is in his lane, and he maneuvers to the left to pass.

*   *   *   *

Officer Jeremy Two Crow is heading east on South Dakota Highway 25 when he picks up the radio microphone, "Officer Two Crow to dispatch."

The radio crackles its tinny response from the female dispatcher, "This is dispatch, go ahead Jeremy."

Jeremy presses the button on the mic, "I've finished the burglary investigation here. I'm just departing Veblen."

"You're still in Veblen?" the voice in the dispatcher's voice whines. "It's almost ten o'clock."

Jeremy smiles as he looks at the dashboard clock. "Correction, it is ten o'clock." Jeremy clicks the mic again, "These guys that got robbed...they are friends of mine. They got their game console taken this afternoon. They went to jumpstart their buddy's, car and when they got back their stuff was gone."

"Roger that," Dispatch replies.

"I'm on the road now," Jeremy sighs as his eyes catch a fast approaching vehicle in his rearview mirror.

"Ten-four. See you when you get back," the dispatcher casually comments.

Gabe's Lexus is a blur as it passes Jeremy's Tahoe. "What the hell?" Jeremy grunts as he flips the switch on his light bar, and the darkness is pierced by the red and blue strobing lights atop his vehicle. He turns the soft rock station out of Fargo off, halting the Pat Monahan crooning of Train's song "Marry Me." He stomps on the gas pedal, putting the Tahoe over eighty miles an hour, then ninety, but not gaining on the car. He reaches for the radio mic. "Dispatch, I'm in pursuit of a gold Lexus sedan, plate number Golf-Foxtrot-4. We are eastbound on Highway 25. Heading toward Claire City."

"Roger that. Running the plate. Be careful," dispatch replies, signing off.

The chase is short lived as a deer gallops from the driver's side ditch onto the road into the path of Jeremy's speeding police unit. "Oh shit!" Jeremy cries out, jamming his foot on the brake and veering to the right. There is nothing that can be done; the deer crunches dead center on the grill. The engine seizes and the disabled Tahoe lurches right. Jeremy struggles to steer the powerless vehicle. The Tahoe bounces over a farm field approach at a much slower speed, but still enough momentum is left in the vehicle to put it on its side. It skids to a sliding stop in the ditch. "God bless America!" Jeremy shouts and pounds his hands on the steering wheel as he hangs belted in his seat. The airbag deployed upon impact and now hangs limply from the steering wheel. "Ahhhh," Jeremy howls in frustration as he disengages his seatbelt and struggles to open the driver's side door against the full weight of gravity on the tipped over vehicle. He finally extricates himself from the wreckage and with his cell phone, he calls the dispatch office. "Hi, Judy, it's Jeremy. I hit a deer." He listens. "No, I'm fine, but I can't say the same for my vehicle. It's dead." He listens again, "Yeah. West of Claire City on 25. I'm in the south ditch. They'll see me."

Chapter 39

Commandeer

BIA Police Station – Sisseton, South Dakota

Charlie sits with Jeremy in the conference room. Stacks of papers are spread out on the table between them. The men go over the details of Jeremy's crash. "You think this is a lot of paperwork?" Charlie asks and Jeremy nods. "It is," Charlie confirms. "I think there are actually fewer forms to fill out if you shoot someone." Charlie points a finger at Jeremy. "Don't get any ideas."

Jeremy laughs, "No, sir."

Charlie scans the dispatch form, the result of the license plate request from Jeremy's initial contact with the speeding vehicle. He shakes his head and sighs, "Why am I not surprised that this involves our friends from the Cities."

Jeremy scratches his chin, "Minnesota plate. Golf, Foxtrot, 4. Gabe Franzen Four. A personalized plate. What an ego on that guy."

"That's some good police work, Jeremy," Charlie nods and casts an approving glance at the police officer across the table. "You got good instincts. Getting that plate in all the commotion. I'm very proud of you."

"Thank you," Jeremy flushes a bit, embarrassed by the compliment. "That means a lot to me." Jeremy leans back in his chair and rubs his chin. "I had no chance. Him in that Lexus, versus me in my Tahoe. I should have never pursued."

The conversation is interrupted as Skip enters the room. He is in blue jeans and a checked western, pearl snap shirt. The officers jump to their feet. "Skip's here!" Charlie almost shouts the words, excited to see his friend. "I guess you got my message."

Handshakes with Skip are warm and hearty. "Had to make sure my rookie was ok."

Jeremy pipes up, "Safe and sound, Boss."

"Good, good. I suppose you'll be needin' a vehicle in the interim."

Charlie flinches. "Sorry, Skip. We kinda commandeered your rig already."

Skip laughs, "That's fine. I'm not gonna need it for awhile."

"How's Betty?" Charlie asks the question he had been dreading ever since he left the voicemail on Skip's answering machine.

A shrug of the shoulders from Skip followed by a shake of his head is the initial response. "No better, no worse. But, I can tell you this, we're both getting tired of the drive to Rochester. It's a long 300 miles."

"What are the doctors saying?" Charlie digs a little deeper.

Skip takes a deep breath. "They're pretty cautious. They always talk like we've beaten it, but..." Skip grimaces, stares down at his shoes, and shakes his head. His eyes well with tears as he meets Charlie's eyes.

Charlie steps forward and puts a hand on Skip's shoulder. "I'm sorry. We're here for you. Whatever you need. Just let us know."

Chapter 40

The Pistol

Charlie LeBeau's Trailer

Claude has accepted the cooking duties for the evening. From his vantage point on the porch, he watches the burgers on the grill as he looks to the west over the Coteau and the clouds moving closer. Claude finishes the grilling chores and ducks back into the house calling out to Charlie, "Burgers are done; come and get 'em!"

Charlie emerges from his bedroom, now in blue jeans and t-shirt, having just arrived home from his shift. "They smell good," Charlie inhales deeply as he fits his belt through its loops.

Claude sets the plate of burgers on the table, and the men finish getting everything else for the meal with no conversation. Claude turns the radio down, lowering the volume on the appropriate mood music from Van Morrison's "Into the Mystic." The haunting tune matches the dreary, threatening weather darkening the sky early this evening. They sit and begin to eat. "It's getting pretty blue to the west," Claude comments between bites of his hamburger. "I wonder if Nat is getting rained out."

"Where they playin' tonight?" Charlie queries, wiping his mouth with a napkin and drinking from his glass of water.

"Groton," Claude replies and almost on cue, the distant rumble of thunder reverberates from far away.

Charlie takes another bite of his burger. "Mmm," he points at what's left on his plate and nods. He swallows and looks to Claude, "Good burgers tonight, Dad."

Thunder again roars in the distance, and both men look out the window at the ever darkening sky. Claude stares at the clouds in the distance. "I bet they got rained out." Claude pushes a bag of potato chips toward Charlie. "You want some more chips?"

Charlie takes another bite and chews, nodding at the offer. He reaches into the bag and extracts a handful of extra crispy chips. Charlie looks across the table at his father. "Dad, I gotta ask you something. Don't get mad."

Claude cocks his head as he looks at Charlie. He finishes chewing and dabs his mouth with a napkin. "Sounds serious. What is it?"

"It's about your pistol. I looked for it the other day. I checked the cigar box in your closet," Charlie pauses and sips from his glass of water before continuing. "I looked where you've always had it, but it wasn't there."

Claude stares at his son and responds with a grunting, "Hmmph."

Charlie fidgets a bit in his chair, returning the glass of water to the table. "I've been dreading this conversation," Charlie sighs as the men stare at each other. "Ever since Nat said Susan had a pistol just like yours," Charlie pauses and takes a deep breath. "You didn't give her your pistol, did you?"

Claude's face is stoic, expressionless, as he pushes away from the table and heads to his bedroom. "Dad!" Charlie calls out as Claude disappears into his bedroom. "Come on, Dad. I told you not to get mad!" he yells.

Claude re-emerges from the bedroom, pistol in hand, marching across the living room. Without a word he sets the Colt Model 1911 pistol on the table as the rumble of closer thunder draws both men's attention to the window. Claude sits back down in his chair and takes a bite of his burger. He chews and meets his son's eyes for a moment before fixing his gaze on the pistol. Swallowing, Claude speaks, calmly, eyes remaining on the gun. "I keep it in my nightstand drawer now. Ever since the deal with Elliot."

Charlie relaxes, suddenly aware of how tense his body had become. He manages a weak smile. Claude turns his attention from the pistol to his son. He shakes his head slightly. "Why would you think I'd give a gun to somebody I barely know?"

Charlie shrugs. "I had to ask. There's a lot of weird stuff going on."

Claude gives a nod toward the pistol. "This piece is an heirloom. It'll be yours someday." Claude leans forward. "I don't need to tell you, that this weapon came in pretty handy in 'Nam."

Charlie holds up a hand in an effort to try to the keep conversation calm. "How are you and Susan?"

Claude flinches, taken aback by the question. "Good. Why?"

Charlie's eyes narrow, and he scratches his head. "That's not the question I really want to ask. I mean...how well do you know her?"

Claude shrugs, slowly comprehending Charlie's line of questioning. "You know I knew her when she was a nun. That was a long time ago. But, really, we're just getting to know each other."

Charlie taps his index finger down on the table for emphasis. "I'm going to tell you something, and this info doesn't go out of this house. Understand?"

Claude frowns. "I understand."

Charlie rubs his chin. "This is strictly between us. I haven't even said anything to anyone in my office, but Susan may have been involved with Father Franzen's death."

"What are you talking about?" Claude reacts defensively. "I have heard you say that he died of a heart attack."

"I know. That's true. I've said that. But, there is more to it than that," Charlie again holds up a hand trying to restrain the conversation. "There was a letter from Susan in his cabin. Plus, ballistics reports indicate it was a pistol, like the one you got there," Charlie gives a nod toward the Colt on the table, "that was fired in the bedroom and on the dock." Charlie again notices the tension in his body, and he relaxes a bit, leaning back in his chair. "The priest had heart issues; it's felt that somebody induced a heart attack with the gunfire."

Claude shakes his head, "I don't believe it!" he responds vehemently. "Have you talked to her?"

"Not officially," Charlie tries to use a soothing tone to calm his father. He points a finger at Claude. "And don't you say anything to her."

Claude deflates in his chair looking to the window and a flash of lightning. His denial of the situation wanes. He nods, capitulating to his son.

Charlie looks at his father. He tries to broker peace by providing additional information. "She knows that I know, or more correctly, that I suspect her. I had early suspicions when Nat snagged her lunch cooler, and we found that .45 caliber ammo." Claude lets his eyes meet his son's for a moment, before he returns his gaze to the window. "Let me clean up. Thanks for cooking tonight, Dad." Charlie stands and begins to clear the table.

Claude gets up from the table as he grabs hold of the pistol. "I'm gonna put this away."

"Sure thing." Charlie gathers another load of items from the table and ferries them to the kitchen counter.

The first few fat raindrops hit the roof of the trailer. Booming thunder rattles the windows as the downpour begins. Claude moves toward his bedroom and stops as the rain roars off the roof. He raises his voice to be heard over the din of the rain, "Gonna be a gully washer of a rain."

"Yup," Charlie replies as he finishes clearing the table.

Chapter 41

Double Tap

BIA Police Station – Sisseton, South Dakota

Charlie rubs his forehead; the first beads of sweat are forming at his hairline. Today is one of those days that you never think of when you decide to become a policeman. No, it's not a gun battle on the street; it's a different kind of battle, a battle of bureaucracy. Charlie sits at his desk reviewing and signing time sheets, the tedious frustration pastes a frown on his face and reddens his cheeks. "If only Skip were back," Charlie whispers as he pulls another form from the stack and marks corrections on it.

The speaker on his desk phone crackles, and Charlie is happy to divert his attention. It is the office administrator, Kathy. "Charlie, sheriff's office. Line one."

Charlie stares at the flickering light of line one. The light is fluttering and twitching, as if indicating an emergency. The ancient phones are wearing out, and the line indicator lights seem to be on their last legs. This gives Charlie a bit of a smile and a moment to relax before answering. He picks up the handset and pushes the button below the glittering red light. "Good morning, this is LeBeau."

Charlie listens. The little bit of smile he had a moment ago is gone. "Oh, geez," is all he can manage into the phone. He sighs. "We'll be right there."

Charlie disconnects the call and pushes another button on the phone to contact Kathy at the front desk. "Hi, Kathy," Charlie speaks calmly into the phone. "Get a hold of Jeremy. Tell him to head to Veblen ASAP. South of town on BIA 10. He'll see the sheriff there." Charlie listens and nods, finishing the conversation he adds, "Thank you," and hangs up.

Charlie stares at his desk a moment and begins shoving papers around. "Dang these papers," Charlie scolds the mess before him out loud. "What the heck did I do with that number?" He lifts the handset of his desk phone, but sets it back in its cradle. He leans back in his chair, extracting his cell phone from his pocket. He scrolls through his phone and finds the number he wants and selects it. "Agent Brown. Two rings and you answer. Wow, I'm impressed at your service."

"I knew it was you, Charlie," Agent Brown replies. "We have caller ID on our phones, believe it or not. I know you don't call unless it's dire, so what's up?"

"Are you back from vacation?" Charlie inquires.

"I'm in my car headin' your way right now," Brown replies.

"Well, step on it," Charlie commands. "We got a body."

"No kidding?" Agent Brown questions with a surprised inflection in his voice.

"Sheriff just called me. A white guy with extra holes in his head," Charlie regrets saying the words, wincing into the phone. "I just got off the phone with him; the Sheriff and a couple deputies are on the scene."

"I'm on my way," Agent Brown says resoundingly.

"It's up in Veblen," Charlie offers. "South of Veblen about a couple miles on the BIA route. See you in a bit."

"I'll see you there," Agent Brown finishes the conversation.

*   *   *   *

Forty-five minutes later, Charlie is parked on the road with the crime scene below him. His vehicle joins a virtual parking lot of other emergency vehicles. Charlie notes the freshness of the air after the storm. It is a little cool and damp, but the summer morning is beautiful. Where he stands, the grade of the road is fifteen to twenty feet above where all the activity is. Yellow police tape extends a couple hundred feet in each direction. From his vantage point, Charlie can make out the outline of what might be a person draped under a white sheet hanging over the fence. It reminds Charlie of a rudimentary Halloween ghost decoration at first glance. The barbed wire fence is tangled with debris along with the body under the sheet. Large sticks and clumps of weeds are tangled in the fence amongst other trash.

The body is about eighty feet downstream from the mouth of the culvert. The overnight rain had swamped the Coteau. The three-quarters of an inch of rain that fell in just a few minutes had flooded this drainage.

Charlie tried to remember if this intermittent stream had a name; Parker Draw is what he thought it was called. The flattened grass and the clear line of demarcation of debris in the fence make it clear where the high-water mark of the storm was.

Charlie looks up at the high cirrus clouds providing a wispy veil of protection from a glaring sun. He nods to himself, thinking that this hazy atmosphere seems appropriate for a murder. Jeremy breaks away from the group surrounding the body and heads up the slope, giving a wave to Charlie still standing on the road grade above, taking in the scene. Sheriff Terry Karst follows Jeremy up the slope. The heavy, black soil oozes through the grass covered slope, and the two men struggle to get to Charlie's position on the road. Jeremy is breathing hard when he makes it to Charlie. "Whew," Jeremy shakes his head and takes a deep breath, thumbs tucked into his utility belt.

"Everything secure?" Charlie questions.

"Yes, sir," Jeremy manages between breaths.

Sheriff Terry Karst manages to make it up the slope. He is in his sixties and has already announced his retirement from law enforcement. He is a man that looks like a sheriff. He's tall and just plain imposing with a dark cowboy hat, dark glasses, and a bushy reddish mustache; he is almost a cartoonish image of law and order. Age shows on the old lawman's face. The lines and grooves along with the varicose veins on his cheeks and nose add to the man's ruddy appearance. "Howdy, Terry," Charlie remarks as he extends his hand.

The sheriff shakes his hand. "Hi, Charlie. It's not a pretty sight down there."

Jeremy looks on in surprise as the much older sheriff's breathing is normal compared to his own gasps from the exertion of coming up the slope. Charlie nods, "The FBI is on the way."

Sheriff Karst provides a wink and a nod, "Good. I'm going to tell everyone down there for the umpteenth time, not to touch anything." He pauses a moment. "Skip still out?"

Charlie nods, and the sheriff eases his way back down the slope.

"We know the victim," Jeremy frowns.

"Really?" Charlie questions, as he starts to carefully work his way down the slope, observing the surroundings. Charlie makes a beeline to the mouth of the culvert first before heading to the group surrounding the body. The modest remnant of the heavy storm flow is nothing more than a trickling stream of water a foot wide and a couple inches deep.

Charlie ambles over to the group of officers around the body. He shakes hands with everyone; all of the Robert's County Sheriff's Deputies are on the scene. Charlie hears one of the deputies make the observation, "Body musta been in the cul-bert."

Charlie can't suppress a smile when he hears the comment. Some of the German families, and also the Norwegians, intermingle the "v" and "b" sounds in their speech. It always gives Charlie a grin.

The crowd of officers parts, and Charlie can approach the body covered by the sheet. Charlie makes eye contact with a deputy and nods; the man pulls back the sheet. Even with the exit wounds mangling the man's face, Charlie recognizes the large man. "Orloski," he breathes the name barely audible to anyone.

"Yeah," Jeremy affirms the identification. He extends his arm, fingers in the form of a pistol. Jeremy's hand and arm recoil twice, as if firing a handgun. "Double tap," he comments dryly, shaking his head and staring at the body strung from the fence. "This was an old school execution. Like the mob."

Chapter 42

Lookie Loos

At the scene of the grisly body discovery, Charlie takes over and tries to lighten the mood. He agrees with the quick conclusion drawn by Jeremy; somebody, likely a fellow mobster, executed Vincent Orloski. Charlie nods to himself as his mind churns over the details of the past couple days and nights. Jeremy hasn't put it together, but Charlie's mind jumps right to the idea that Gabe Franzen's license plate, identified by Jeremy before he smacked a deer, was not a coincidence to this crime.

Charlie raises his hands. "Listen up!" he calls out, and the conversations among the officers cease. He lowers his arms. "Well, boys, I think we're off the hook on this one. FBI is going to be here. I talked to an agent before I left the office, and they were headed our way." Charlie's hands go to his hips, his thumbs find his utility belt, and he relaxes as he continues, "I'm sure the Feds will love to sink their teeth into an organized crime hit."

Jeremy is puzzled. He casts an inquisitive glance at Charlie. "What's that leave for us?"

Charlie shrugs, "Guard duty. Keep the area secure until the FBI and the DCI investigators say different." Charlie points to the roadway above them where several passersby have parked their cars and stand on the shoulder of the road looking on curiously at all the activity. Charlie taps Jeremy on the shoulder. He doesn't take his eyes off the gathering crowd. "Make sure you keep watch on the lookie-loos. I don't want this crime scene contaminated. Agent Brown is cranky enough, and I don't want to get my butt chewed by him over some compromised evidence."

Jeremy nods and moves up the slope toward the crowd. Charlie calls out to Sheriff Karst, "Hey, Terry, can you spare a couple deputies for awhile to secure the scene?"

The sheriff pushes his dark glasses back in place with a single finger on the nose piece. "It would be my pleasure. Duke, Kyle. You're on guard duty with Charlie. He'll tell you when you can go."

"Thanks, Terry," Charlie shakes the Sheriff's hand.

"See you later. Let me know if you need anything else," Sheriff Karst moseys up the slope toward his cruiser.

Charlie watches the sheriff move past the crowd, waving at a few people and acknowledging a few others with a pointed finger. Ever the consummate politician, Charlie thinks to himself. Charlie spies a couple of familiar faces in the crowd, now restrained by plastic yellow crime scene tape that Jeremy has erected along the shoulder of the gravel road. Veronica and Susan wave as they notice Charlie looking in their direction. Charlie smiles and heads up the slope.

The bulk of the officers have broken up their gathering. The two deputies assigned by the sheriff stand near the body. They watch the growing crowd of people and cars clog the narrow gravel road. Charlie gives a wave to the two deputies as he heads up the slope to catch up to Veronica and Susan. Charlie breaks off his route to the two women and heads to his Tahoe instead. He motions to Veronica to meet him at his vehicle, and the women back away from the police tape restraint and move through the crowd toward Charlie's Tahoe parked on the shoulder of the road. "Good morning," Charlie smiles as the women approach.

Veronica leans in for a hug from Charlie and immediately begins her questions, "Hi, Charlie. What happened?"

Charlie waves to Susan, acknowledging her presence and receives an impatient smile from the woman, who waits anxiously for an answer to Veronica's question. "It was all over the police scanner," Veronica rattles off her statement. "We had to close the office and come up to see what's going on."

"Off the record?" Charlie begins with his usual question to his reporter girlfriend.

"Of course," Veronica tilts her head, annoyed at the constant, routine question from her beau.

"Gangsters," Charlie says matter-of-factly.

"Gangsters?" Veronica and Susan question simultaneously.

"Shhh," Charlie hushes the women with a frown. "Not so loud."

Charlie can't help but smile at the priceless, quizzical expressions of both women. "Organized crime out of the Twin Cities...at least that's our preliminary conclusion."

"It was a hit?" Veronica questions further.

"Looks like it," Charlie purses his lips. "A body dump at the minimum." He glances back and forth between the women, "Good enough?"

"Yeah, we'll get out of your hair in a minute, "Veronica offers. "Just wanted a couple of pictures for the latest edition."

Charlie holds up a finger, "All this...off the record."

"I know!" Veronica growls through gritted teeth, that can't hold back a smile.

Veronica fumbles with her camera, and Charlie puts on a serious expression, trying get one more dig in on her. "One thing that I can go on the record with..." He pauses and both women look longingly at LeBeau, awaiting a juicy comment. Charlie stoically points to the fence line, "Underneath that sheet...there's a dead body."

Veronica and Susan roll their eyes and sigh in disgust as Charlie laughs at his joke; the gallows humor is very much under appreciated by the non-law enforcement women.

Chapter 43

Coteau Vista

By the time Federal Bureau of Investigation Agent Austin Brown arrives at the murder scene south of Veblen, the curiosity of the public has waned. No civilians are left to crowd the gravel road; however, the shoulder of the road is still thick with DCI and FBI technicians gathering crime scene evidence. It looks like a small town is springing up on the rural road. Agent Brown locates Charlie in his vehicle, "Long day, Sergeant LeBeau?"

Charlie is in the middle of a yawn as the agent catches him by surprise. Brown laughs, and Charlie can't help but laugh with him as he dismounts from his vehicle and shakes the FBI agent's hand. "Yes, it's been a long day of standing around waiting for you guys," Charlie laughs again. "I'm reminded of my days in the army...hurry up and wait."

Agent Brown nods; he looks to the west and takes in the tree-covered hills of the Coteau. He turns his attention to the east, looking past the crime scene tape; Brown absorbs the green valley below him. "It's pretty up here," Brown smiles enjoying the views. "I don't think I've ever been up on this part of the reservation." He sweeps his hand toward the hills then back to the valley. "It's got everything, a Coteau vista and a valley view."

Charlie nods, "You're right. It's funny; I take it for granted. It seems like I barely notice it anymore unless somebody points it out."

"Gotta stop and smell the roses, Charlie," Agent Brown's statement is more of a command as he slaps his hand on Charlie's shoulder.

"What do you think?" Charlie inquires. "Can I let my guys go home?"

It's Agent Brown's turn to yawn, and he stretches his arms and back. "I'm sorry, long drive today."

Brown leans against the Tahoe, and Charlie flinches. "Don't get your suit dirty; my vehicle's kinda muddy."

Brown waves away the warning as he looks at his muted gray suit. "Ahhh, don't worry about it." He looks down from the shoulder of the road at all the activity below him. "Yeah, we can handle it from here. Go ahead and let your guys go. I'm guessin' we'll be here through the night and tomorrow." The FBI agent looks north toward Veblen then south along the road. "I can't imagine that anyone is going to bother us out here in the middle of nowhere. Yeah, send your guys home."

Charlie nods, and the men stand in silence a few moments observing the investigation. Men and women in blue windbreakers with FBI printed on the back scurry about. "So," Charlie breaks the silence, "what are they saying?"

"Who?" Brown replies.

"Your bosses, what are they saying?" Charlie clarifies.

Agent Brown stifles a chuckle. "First thing they said was, 'What the hell is going on out on that reservation.' Then..." Brown gestures toward the crowd of investigators, "you can see what happened next." The FBI agent takes a deep breath and shakes his head slowly, "When they heard our victim was Orloski, all hell broke loose. This is going to rattle some cages in Minneapolis. Did you know this guy was counsel to Carl Franzen?"

"Orloski? He was a lawyer?" Charlie asks, his expression crinkling his nose in surprise. Brown nods in affirmation. Charlie shakes his head, not comprehending. "I'm not going to try to pretend to understand the workings of organized crime, but this is too weird. Orloski was basically babysitting Gabe Franzen out here."

"Any idea where Gabe is?" Brown inquires.

"None what-so-ever," Charlie replies. "But, I'm pretty sure he's involved with all this." Charlie nods and turns his eyes toward the group of investigators hovering over the body still entangled in the barbed wire fence.

"Do you know anything about the Franzen crime family?" Brown cocks his head and looks at Charlie as he asks the question.

"No, and I'm afraid to ask," Charlie whispers the words, a little frightened of what he might hear.

The FBI agent's eyes widen, and his eyebrows arch. "You don't wanna know, but I'm going to tell you anyway. Franzen's crew has been linked to seventy, that's seven zero, murders in the last five years."

"In the Twin Cities?" Charlie softly questions.

"Yeah," Brown affirms with a nod. "Some Chicago crime families have sensed weakness in the Minneapolis area, so they've been puttin' the moves on Franzen's territory. In turn, Franzen's been sending a steady message."

Charlie emits a low whistle in disbelief and amazement. "Seventy bodies? Glad the FBI's got job security." Charlie laughs, "I'll keep to my quiet life on the reservation, thank you very much."

"So much for quiet," Brown frowns and waves a hand at the investigators still photographing the scene. "You're in the thick of it now, just like us." He shakes his head and continues, "I got five more agents from the Minneapolis office en route. They'll be here tomorrow to scour every square inch of this creek and all the evidence associated with this case." Brown begins to nod. "They'll have this thing wrapped up pretty quick."

Charlie jerks his head in the direction of the stream. "Come on, I want to show you something."

Agent Brown pushes himself away from the Tahoe and follows Charlie down the slope. "Careful in this mud," Charlie cautions the agent. "Especially you and your fancy shoes."

"I'll have you know," Brown takes an argumentative tone, "I've been wearing oxford shoes like these for fifteen years on the job, and I've never had any trouble navigating any terrain." The agent punctuates his statement with a yell, "Whoa!" as he slips down the slope falling, but catching and protecting himself and his suit by planting both hands into the muddy grass.

Charlie shakes his head, "You can't say I didn't warn you."

The agent grins, embarrassed by the situation. He pushes himself up and looks around. Nobody seems to have noticed as all the other investigators are engrossed in their work. He scrapes mud from his fingers as he follows Charlie to the mouth of the culvert. "Pretty graceful there, Fred Astaire," Charlie mocks his friend as they step out of the mud and onto the smooth surface of the concrete box culvert.

Agent Brown grins, still embarrassed. Charlie shines a flashlight into the box and walks to what is about the middle of the culvert. "Big culvert," Brown notes his voice echoing in the tunnel-like structure. "I bet a lot of water came through here last night."

"Yeah," Charlie shines his light on the barely trickling ribbon of water on the bottom of the culvert. "Do you think you can manage not to slip again and fall into the current?"

"Oh, you're hilarious," Brown replies with just a touch of sarcasm.

Charlie squats down and Brown follows suit. "I thought this was a body dump." Charlie touches a nick on the concrete floor of the culvert with his finger, then moves to another scuff on the smooth surface. "Then I noticed these."

Agent Brown touches the divots that are just a few inches apart, nodding, he doesn't say anything. Standing he extends his arm; hand and fingers in the shape of a pistol, index finger pointing toward the divots. His arm jerks twice as if firing a pistol. Looking upstream for a moment, then downstream, Brown can see people in blue windbreakers crossing back and forth out of the stream. "He was killed right here. Just a coincidence the rain washed the body out in the storm last night. Bad luck for the killer."

Charlie stands and points to the upstream fence that holds its share of debris, "Yeah, the fence is intact on the upstream side, so the body didn't come from up there," He turns and points to the outlet. "No, Orloski was killed here. Slugs probably got washed down aways."

Agent Brown nods slowly. He extends an arm and slaps Charlie on the back. "That's some pretty good police work, Charlie. I'll get some men with metal detectors. With any luck, we can recover those slugs and get a match to something in our data base."

"There's something else," Charlie tries to say it quietly, but his voice echoes in the chamber.

"Oh, yeah?" Brown's curiosity is piqued.

"Let's go back to my truck," Charlie motions the agent to follow him. "I don't want what I'm saying echoing all over."

The men exit the upstream side of the culvert, away from the crowd of investigators. Carefully maneuvering up the slope, to avoid a muddy mishap, Charlie and the agent make it to the road surface and to Charlie's Tahoe. "Get in," Charlie orders to the agent.

Inside the Tahoe, Charlie shuffles through some folders in his backpack on the armrest between the driver and passenger seat. Finally finding the correct folder, he hands it to Agent Brown. "We had an incident near here the other night. My rookie officer hit a deer just east of Veblen on Highway 25."

Agent Brown holds the closed folder at arms length, a puzzled look creases his face. "So?"

"I pulled that file this morning," Charlie taps the file. "I knew you'd want to see it."

"You're telling me what's in this folder," Brown mumbles as he opens the manila folder, "has something to do with our body?"

"If you look at the report," Charlie again taps the folder, "you'll see that my officer was returning from a routine call. It was dark, and he was passed by a vehicle. The officer estimated the vehicle was traveling well over one hundred miles an hour."

Agent Brown skims the report as he listens to Charlie. "Gabe Franzen?" Agent Brown looks at Charlie for a moment, before turning his attention back to the report.

Charlie continues, "My officer, he's got young, good eyes. He got the plate."

"Gabe was up here a couple nights ago," Brown shakes his head and turns his attention to the undulating hills where the sun is starting to make its way. "It's still a beautiful view up here." Brown looks at the report again, before closing the folder. "Too much of a coincidence." Brown glances to his left and sees Charlie nodding.

The men sit in silence a few moments before Brown speaks up, "I don't know what to tell you Charlie." Agent Brown scans the hills in the distance.

Charlie stares toward the horizon. "You don't have to tell me anything, just get 'im."

Agent Brown nods and continues to stare at the Coteau to the west.

Chapter 44

Sica Hollow

Sica Hollow State Park – South Dakota

Claude and Susan hike in the cool morning air. The damp environment holds pockets of fog, as differing temperature layers trap humidity from the recent rain. "I'm so glad you called me to see the park. I have never been here, even in my first go round in Sisseton as a nun."

"How about the pronunciation, *See-chee* Hollow, as opposed to the way it's spelled. My mind struggles with it whenever I see it written or even on the highway signs on the drive out," Claude offers.

Sica Hollow State Park consists of about thousand acres tucked into the eastern side-slope of the Coteau des Prairies. Just a short, twenty-five minute road trip west and a little north from Sisseton, you'll find a peaceful woodland setting for camping, hiking, and horseback riding. Autumn is the peak for visitation as crowds come to enjoy the bold colors of the turning leaves, but Sica Hollow is a hidden gem tucked away in northeastern South Dakota any time of the year.

"This ground fog is spooky," Susan comments as she makes her way along a marked trail.

"After a rain is always the best time to visit," Claude offers. "Hardly anyone else comes out here when it's wet, and it's like a whole different world in the forest, freshly rinsed." Claude inhales deeply, "Ahhh, smell that musty musk!"

The sun works to burn away the mist trapped in the trees, and the pair continues to hike. "What do you think?" Claude continues. "Should we go to the top?"

Susan nods and Claude leads the way up the sloping trail. They stop on a rickety wooden foot bridge and observe red-tinted, watery mud oozing from the hillside. Claude smiles and shakes his head and Susan notices. "What's so funny?"

"The history of this area is funny to me."

"What do you mean?" Susan questions.

Claude rubs his chin, "I'm sure you've heard the stories about this place. It's haunted. It's mystical."

Susan nods, "Yeah."

"All those legends...the legends associated with this site, like how spirits gathered here. Those stories scared a lot of Indians and kept them away. Still do. You ask a lot of Indians in Sisseton, and they'll tell you they've never been here. Their parents forbid them to visit." Claude points at the red, liquefied mud draining to the puddle below them as they stand on the boardwalk. "You see that red mud?"

"Yes," Susan nods.

"That was blood to the old Indian people. It scared them," Claude chuckles. "But, what does science tell us now? It tells us that iron in the soils was deposited by the glaciers ten thousand years ago, that iron is what leaches into the shallow aquifer and makes the stream sometimes run red. The truth is boring. It's kind of a let down," Claude grimaces as he stares at the mud.

Susan laughs, "You'd rather it be the blood of your people?"

"Maybe," Claude's eyes light up, "now that would be interesting."

The couple strolls single file on the soft trail. A wild turkey with her chicks darts across the trail ahead of them, and Claude silently points the birds out to Susan. The birds disappear into the lush vegetation as the pair continues on their way. "This reminds me of a rainforest," Susan finally speaks after walking in silence a few minutes. "We seem like we are ten thousand miles from Sisseton. It's like an Amazon rainforest."

"You've seen the Amazon?" Claude inquires.

Susan laughs, a bit embarrassed, "No, but this is kind of what I imagine it would be."

Claude shakes his head with a melancholy grin. "I saw the jungle in Vietnam. I can definitely see a resemblance. But, I will say this; I'm not terrified of what's hidden in these bushes over here like I was over there." Claude laughs.

They reach the summit and can look to the east, over the tops of the trees and see the farm fields below. To the west the rolling hills are covered in grass and are partitioned here and there by fences. "What do you think?" Claude poses the question. "Back through the jungle, to the car?"

Susan grabs Claude's hand. "Let's go. I'm hungry and our picnic lunch awaits."

The sun finally burns through the remaining fog, and the forest steams with humidity. The birds begin chirping and singing as the forest comes alive with the sun shining through. There is a little conversation as the two tread carefully down the trail. Twenty minutes later, Susan pops the trunk of her car and Claude grabs the cooler and a large cloth bag with loops for handles, full of picnic supplies. Susan spreads a table cloth on the picnic table shielded from the sun by a large oak tree. Sandwiches are handed out and lunch begins in earnest. "I think I'm ready to move on," Susan remarks between bites of turkey and Swiss cheese on a croissant.

"I suspected as much," Claude nods and looks at the woman across the table from him. He reaches out his hand, and she places hers in his.

"Really?" she replies, surprised by Claude's comment. She pats his hand and grasps her sandwich for another bite.

Claude smiles. "I got a real earful from Charlie the other night. We were having supper and suddenly I get the third degree." Claude takes a bite, and Susan watches and waits for him to continue. "That son of mine questioned me about my Colt pistol. He had snooped around my room looking for it."

Susan smiles at Claude. "I'm not worried about Charlie...or the law. Whatever was done was done...whoever did it." She stares at Claude for a moment and takes another bite of her sandwich and washes it down with a diet cola.

Claude frowns. "It doesn't have to be justified to me. I'm glad he's dead. I was there. I know what that guy did. I've lived with guilt all these years." Claude shakes his head and sips from his soda. "Justice if you ask me. Delayed far, far too long, but justice nonetheless."

Claude holds up his soda in a toast. "To justice."

Susan clinks her aluminum can off of Claude's. "Justice." They tip their sodas and drink. Susan sets her can down and bites into her sandwich. She reaches for the potato chips. "I know we understand it. It took thirty years for this stuff to see the light of day." She pauses, her face pasted with a frown. She finally continues. "A lot of people don't get it and don't want to. The Church is very powerful...was powerful. All these accusations and lawsuits were inevitable."

Claude holds up a hand, "Yeah, it's just that...Charlie thought I had loaned you my gun."

"Oh," Susan frowns, eyes narrowing in serious thought. "He's just looking out for you. That's only natural. It's funny, what a coincidence that we both have the same kind of pistol. He thought there might be evidence that leads back to you. Does anyone really know how many pistols the same as we have that are out there in the general population? U.S. Army Officer issued pistols, those Colt .45s? There are probably thousands. Charlie's just trying to make sure he can protect you."

Claude shrugs. "I guess, as if I need protecting." He can't suppress a knowing smile.

"I often think about when my uncle gave me his Korean War Colt. Just before he died...it was funny. I always thought, 'What am I going to do with a pistol?' but he knew I was alone and could use something for protection." Susan puts her hands up in the air. "I just hope I never have to use it for real." Susan clucks her tongue, and her expression reflects a melancholy mood as she sighs.

"I've enjoyed your stay." Claude smiles a sad smile.

"Same here." Susan reflects Claude's smile.

They nibbles on chips and finish their sandwiches in silence, listening to the birds singing in the nearby trees. Claude finally speaks, "What are you gonna tell Veronica?"

Susan signs, "I'll just tell her thanks. Thanks for the chance to pretend to be a journalist."

Claude nods. "She's a nice woman. She'll understand. Once she figures it out, and she will, Charlie'll tell her. She'll understand."

Claude hoists his soda again to toast, "Here's to a little more time together!"

Susan raises her can, "Cheers!"

Chapter 45

Cheshire Cat

BIA Police Station – Sisseton, South Dakota

Another day of paperwork keeps Charlie at his desk. It is a moment's reprieve when Skip, dressed in street clothes, walks through the door with bluster. "Sheesh, I step away a couple weeks, and all hell breaks loose!"

Charlie looks up from his paperwork and springs to his feet, his frown turning to a smile. "Come on, man, do you gotta come in here and rub it in?"

Charlie steps forward and shakes Skip's hand. "You know I do," Skip shrugs and smiles.

"What's with you?" Charlie questions, backing up suspiciously and giving Skip the side eye. "You look like the cat that swallowed a canary, or what's that cat from Alice in Wonderland?"

"The Cheshire Cat?" Skip asks.

"Yeah, that's the one," Charlie smiles. "The cat that seems a little too satisfied."

"I don't have much to smile about, but seeing you doing all that paperwork on top of the fact that I may be getting used to seeing what retirement might be like…now that makes me smile." Skip inhales deeply and lets his breath out slowly. "Yup, I could get used to this." He flips a hand toward Charlie. "Look at you. You in charge. You are a natural. Sounds like you've got everything wrapped up. The priest, the kids, a gangster…everything figured out. It looks more and more like I don't need to come back."

Charlie frowns. "Don't say that. I need you." There's a pleading tone to Charlie's voice. "The paperwork, the overtime, timesheets…I've barely held a fishing pole in my hands this summer." Charlie throws his hands in the air. "Please don't do this to me."

Skip's smile flips like a switch to a frown. "It's not up to me."

"I'm sorry, Skip..." Charlie sees Skip's eyes well with tears. "I didn't' mean..." he stammers, "How's Betty doing?"

"Doctors say she's doing better," Skip's head shakes contradicting his words. "She tells me the chemo is gonna kill her, not the cancer. But, that's what all the doctors say. They try to poison the body just the right amount to get rid of the cancer, but the side effects..."

Charlie nods, "I know."

"I'm sorry, Charlie," Skip covers his heart with his hand, "You know all about it, your sister...your mom." Skip rubs his face, pinching the bridge of his nose, "It's not good, Charlie. She's talking about arrangements now. Flowers. Who's gonna sing at the funeral." Skip shakes his head. "Who am I to stop her from taking a pragmatic approach? I want her to be happy."

The men stand in silence as the harsh reality of life and death blankets the room. "Hey," Skip's voice rises to a shout, "I'm not here to talk personal stuff, well, maybe just a little personal business." He holds his thumb and forefinger together, narrowing his eyes as he gazes at the narrow gap between his digits. "The real reason I stopped by was I need a welfare check on my Uncle Titus up in Veblen. I've been trying to get a hold of him, and he won't answer his phone."

"Why don't you go? Take Betty up for a drive?" Charlie asks.

Skip shakes his head. "You know how Titus is. He doesn't like to think he is being babysat."

Charlie's head bobs. "Sure. It'll give me a chance to run by the culvert and see if our FBI buddies have cleared out."

Skip extends his hand. "Thanks, Charlie. I really appreciate all you're doing."

Charlie firmly grips his friend's hand. "It's no problem. You hang in there."

Chapter 46

Uncle Titus

Charlie LeBeau drives north of Sisseton under the bright sunshine and clear, blue sky accentuated with a few cumulus clouds. He turns west at Claire City noticing the growing crops aided by the recent rain. The drive gives Charlie the feeling he is able to take a breath after a hectic week. He smiles as the AM radio station plays "Sukiyaki" by Kyu Sakamota, and he turns up the volume. The lilting Japanese love song induces Charlie to hum along. He has a new appreciation for Skip's work as police captain, and his desire to attain such a position is diminishing quickly. Fields of green, corn and soybeans flank the highway. Charlie whispers aloud, "Looks like another record breaking crop this year...should be some big deer this fall."

On the south side of Veblen, the reservation housing sits in orderly fashion with symmetrical driveways and square, uniform houses of the same, repetitive design. The subdivision is shabby and unkempt looking in comparison to the private residences of the community where mature trees line the streets and Kentucky blue grass grows in the yards. The houses here are all thirty plus years old, but they look weathered enough to be eighty. Charlie locates Titus' house and parks on the street. He makes his way to the front porch of the tribal government housing project residence. The area where a lawn would be is nothing more than exposed soil and a few scattered kochia weeds thriving in the environment. Plastic grocery bags flutter in the wind, snagged on last year's spindly crop of weeds. The most notable object on the lawn is a 1980s Dodge sedan up on blocks and missing all doors. It sits like a statue on display in the front yard, growing a rusty patina, exchanging the faded blue paint for a corroded metal finish. Charlie notes that the rust has definitely taken the majority of the territory on the body of the old car, a noticeable victory for the rust since his last visit three years prior.

Charlie observes the blinds are closed, and he remembers from previous visits this is a good sign, as Titus tended to like to keep it cool and dark. Charlie raps on the door sharply with his knuckles, followed with a shout, "Titus, it's Charlie LeBeau!"

He tries the handle of the door, but it is locked. Charlie detects a shuffling inside the door, and the deadbolt clicks. The door opens wide, exposing Titus Korman, a slight, stooped, wrinkled man, sporting a shock of gray hair. The old man squints into the brightness of the outdoors. "What do you want, Charlie LeBeau? Did my neighbors call the police again? I told them I thought their dog was a coyote. It scared my cat, so I took a shot at it. So what?"

Charlie is taken aback by the defensive barrage of words the old man immediately spews, but quickly smiles and laughs. "No, sir. We can talk about that some other time. Can I come in for a moment?"

"Come on in," Titus waves his hand. "I got some coffee."

Charlie enters, closing the door behind him. The modest home is tidy with the aroma of fresh brewed coffee permeating the air. "Let me open some curtains and get some light in here."

Titus shuffles around the room, opening blinds and curtains. "I like to keep it cool and not have to run the air conditioner, so pardon the darkness a moment." With a couple windows yielding now to the sunlight, Titus declares, "That's good enough."

The sunlight exposes a black and white cat perched on the back of the couch. It eyes Charlie suspiciously for a moment before bolting off the couch and disappearing into a back room. Titus laughs as he watches the cat scamper away. "Old Chompers, he's scared of people. It's pretty much always just him and me in this house." Titus points a finger at Charlie. "Please take no offense that he ran out of here. That cat is the reason I shot at the neighbor's dog, like I was just sayin'. Heck, I missed on purpose; I was just trying to scare him."

"You're not in trouble about the dog, it's not about that, Titus. Skip's worried about ya. You don't answer your phone."

Titus shuffles to the table that holds the phone. He picks up the handset of the cordless phone. "Dang battery is dead. I haven't been able to get a new battery yet. It's been down a couple days."

"Oh, ok," Charlie is relieved that this problem can be easily rectified. "Do you have an old regular phone packed away someplace? You know, the old kind that don't need batteries?"

Titus slaps the heel of his hand to his forehead. "By the ghost of Drifting Goose!" he exclaims. "I never even thought of that. I got one in the back I can plug in. You're one sharp detective there, Charlie LeBeau."

Charlie blushes as Titus shuffles by him to a backroom. Charlie looks around the living room, noticing that the old man seems to have everything in order. Looking back toward the hallway and the back room, he sees Chompers emerge, slink to the couch and climb back to his perch on the back of the sofa. The cat peers outside then back to the stranger in the living room. Charlie can't help but think of his earlier conversation with Skip about the Cheshire Cat. This cat seemed to be another example of a smirking kitty.

Charlie hears the familiar noise of sliding closet doors open and close. From the back room Titus shouts, "I got it!" The old man emerges, holding an old style office phone with push buttons and a curly cord to the handset. "I'll get this plugged in, and I'll be back in business."

"Let me help you," Charlie offers. He unplugs the cordless receiver and snaps the phone cable into the old style phone.

Titus picks up the receiver. "Got a dial tone!" the old man grins.

"Good," Charlie offers a congratulatory smile. "You give Skip a call and let him know you are alright."

"Sure thing," Titus confirms.

"I'll be going now," Charlie announces loud enough to get the cat's attention for a moment. He points a finger at the old man and smiles. "No more shootin' at dogs."

The old man grins slyly and chuckles, "I won't...unless they need shootin'!"

Charlie laughs, "Lock the door behind me, Titus. Goodbye."

"Will do. Take care, Charlie LeBeau." Charlie exits, and Titus closes the door behind the policeman.

On the porch, Charlie listens to the satisfying click of the deadbolt. He looks around at the neighbors. The bright sunshine gives Charlie pause, and he dons his sunglasses. There is no sign of activity in the three block vicinity of the housing project comprised of about twenty homes. Finally, a dog trots by about fifty yards down the street, oblivious to Charlie's presence. It is a German shepherd mix. Charlie whistles, the dog stops, sees Charlie, and bolts away, continuing on what seems to be a predetermined chore. Charlie marches to his Tahoe, satisfied that the day can be considered at least partially successful.

Chapter 47

The Clue

Veblen, South Dakota

After his visit with Uncle Titus, it's another "welfare check" of another variety for Charlie. He heads south of Veblen on BIA Route 10 at a leisurely pace in his Tahoe. Gravel kicks up and ticks off the chassis of the Chevy four-wheel drive vehicle. In a few minutes, he arrives at the site of the box culvert where Orloski's body was discovered. The operation is a shell of itself from the previous day. Charlie slows to an idle as he passes two generic sedans and a van, all with federal government plates, parked on the side of the road. At the bottom of the grade, on the flattest spot in the ditch, a small shade is erected; a group of five men and women in blue jeans and blue windbreakers relax on folding chairs. Charlie rolls down his window and waves as he idles on by. A couple of the group's members wave nonchalantly back to him, and Charlie has seen enough of the murder site. He presses on the accelerator and continues south, back toward South Dakota Highway 10.

Charlie's mind wanders a bit as he thinks of his chances of actually going fishing this weekend and where they might be biting. The distraction is short-lived, as just a couple of miles from the culvert, he spies a teenage Indian boy walking on the side of the road, coming toward him. "What's this about?" Charlie questions aloud as he brakes to a stop next to the boy dressed in long, baggy shorts, a black t-shirt with what appears to be a rock band logo "MEGA-kill" in white letters on the black fabric. The young man is rail-thin. His spiked-hair is short and glistens in the sun, covered in some sort of gel-product. "What's the problem?" Charlie inquires.

"No problem," the boy responds as he halts. "Just walking to Veblen."

"Why you walkin'?" Charlie's eyes squint a bit as he sizes up the boy, trying to rack his memory in hopes of recalling who this teen might be. "Car trouble?"

"We ran out of gas."

Charlie nods, "Hop in. I'll give you a ride."

"That's ok. Thanks though," the boy points to the north. "It's just a couple miles. I don't want to be a bother."

"It's more like four or five miles," Charlie beckons the boy, "Just hop in. It's not a problem. Protect and serve. Today I serve," Charlie grins as he puts the vehicle in park, and the doors unlock.

The young man purses his lips as he looks north and shrugs, finally nodding. He heads to the passenger side of the vehicle and gets in. Charlie puts the truck in gear and turns around with a wide turn, edging off the shoulder a bit, causing Evan to grip the armrest in a spasm of fear. "What's your name?" Charlie asks. His memory has failed him.

"Evan McGill," his voice rising, as if in questioning his own name.

"Oh, Cecilia's boy?" Charlie presses.

"Yeah."

"You play any ball?" Charlie continues his questions as they head north.

"Not this summer," Evan replies in a monotone as he stares forward.

"I'm talking basketball, not baseball. You seem tall and wiry. You must play.

"Not since seventh grade."

"Why not? You should think about it. I bet you can play. I went to high school with your mom, and she could hoop."

Charlie pulls into Grobe's and accompanies Evan to the cash register, where they borrow a gas can. "We'll be right back," Charlie informs the young lady at the counter.

Charlie puts five dollars worth of fuel into the can and straps it to the roof of his Tahoe. In a few minutes they pass by the crime scene again, and Charlie waves at the investigators. After a few minutes of one-sided conversation, with Charlie unable to pry much from the boy, they are upon the teenager's car. The ancient Subaru station wagon is pulled onto the shoulder, and Charlie eases his Tahoe to within an inch of its bumper as he observes two teenage boys scramble to right their reclined seats inside the car. The vehicle has caught them by surprise and when they notice it is a law enforcement vehicle, they react. "Your friends?" Charlie grins at Evan as they watch the spastic actions of the car's occupants trying to get out of the vehicle.

Evan nods, frowning with disgust. "Who are they?" Charlie asks as he opens his car door.

"Kevin Drapeaux and Benny Crawford."

The two boys are outside the car, waiting as Charlie pulls the gas can from the roof of the Tahoe and moves to fill up the Subaru's tank. They look like they are a little older than Evan. Both are dressed in shorts and plain white t-shirts. One has shoulder length hair, and the other has longer hair in a braid. Evan has made it from the passenger side and has the car's gas cap off, ready for Charlie to dump the fuel in. "Hello, boys," Charlie smiles at his audience as he tips up the gas can.

"Hello, sir and, hi," are mumbled by the latest additions to the conversation.

As Charlie pours the gasoline into the tank, he can't help but notice the back of the station wagon. Inside the cargo area is a scattered mess of miscellaneous items, but a couple things catch his eye, two video game consoles as well as multiple controllers.

The gas can is empty, and Charlie turns to the boy with the braid, "Try 'er."

The oldest boy jumps into the car, and Charlie notices that he is wearing new and very expensive basketball shoes. The engine turns over after a few hesitations.

"All right, boys, I'll be on my way," Charlie hands the gas can to Evan. "Make sure you return this." Charlie looks at the boys, pulls out his wallet and thumbs out a bill. "Here's another five to get some gas in Veblen. You guys owe me ten bucks." Charlie hands the money to Evan. "Evan, think about what I said about playing ball."

Charlie moves to his Tahoe, opening the door he gives a last look at the boys still milling around as they decide who gets to ride where in the little car. "See you around."

Evan gives a wave and ducks into the front passenger seat.

*　　*　　*　　*

In the Tahoe, Charlie grabs his notepad and pen. He jots down the license of the Subaru and the names of the boys as he shakes his head. "Jeremy's gonna love this."

The Subaru backs up and pulls around the Tahoe heading north to Veblen. Charlie gives a wave again to the boys as he puts his vehicle in gear and heads south.

*   *   *   *

Back at the station it's the end of a long day for Charlie as he eyes 6:00 p.m. on the wall clock. He waited for Jeremy to come in and start his shift to be able to talk to him in person. Charlie enters the locker room where Jeremy is changing into his uniform. "Hey, Boss," Jeremy smiles. "Busy day?"

Charlie shakes his head, "Not really. Any plans for the night?"

Jeremy frowns. "Nah. Just some traffic patrol. Ticket book is still pretty heavy." Jeremy's frown goes to a smile, "Eh, we'll see what comes across the radio."

Charlie reaches into his pocket, removing his notebook. "Well, I got something you'll be interested in."

Jeremy stops what he's doing, shirt half-buttoned, intrigued by Charlie's statement and tone. Charlie copies the names and license plate number onto another sheet in his notepad. He tears it off with a flourish. "Here you go," he says, handing the paper to Jeremy.

Jeremy eyes the note. "What's this?"

"It's a clue. I'm pretty sure this is about your rash of stolen video games."

Jeremy flinches. "Seriously? These are the guys?"

Charlie nods. "Talk to Evan first. Go easy on him, he's just a boy. I think he'll give up the other two, but I want the kid glove treatment for him. I know his mom."

"Whatever you say, Boss. Thanks." Jeremy shoves the note in his pocket and finishes buttoning his shirt as Charlie turns to leave. "You going out?"

"Nat's got a game. I'll see you later."

Jeremy is all smiles with the information in his pocket. "All right then, have fun. See you tomorrow."

Chapter 48

Confession

Sisseton Baseball Complex

The game is underway as Claude and Charlie watch from the bleachers. Nat winds and tosses a fastball low in the dirt. "Is Susan coming?" Charlie turns to ask Claude the question between pitches.

"Far as I know," Claude responds, not taking his eyes off Nat winding and throwing another ball. "They're working on a deadline, but I think Veronica and Susan will be here later. Maybe we can all go to the casino for a late supper?"

"I don't know, Dad, it might be kind of late."

"We'll see," Claude pronounces definitively, leaving a late supper open for future debate.

Nat pitches and coaxes a ground ball to the shortstop, who throws the runner out at first. Claude and Charlie cheer as the teams exchange positions on the field. After the pitcher has had his warm up tosses, the leadoff hitter for Sisseton steps to the plate. Claude clears his throat. "Hey, Charlie, I wanted to talk to you about Susan."

"Yeah, about what?" Charlie watches the Watertown hurler fire a pitch at the knees across the plate for a called strike.

"Actually," Claude cocks his head as he looks at Charlie, "she wants to talk to you. I'm sort of paving the way."

Charlie is only half paying attention to Claude's conversation as he watches the action on the field; the Sisseton batter fouls a pitch straight back. "Talk to me about what?" Charlie asks again softly.

"I think you know," Claude mumbles the words.

Charlie turns his attention to his dad, "This about the priest?"

"Yeah."

Charlie shrugs. "That's fine, I guess. She wanna come to the station? Meet for lunch? Or what?"

"Why don't you just ask her when she gets to the game tonight?"

Charlie watches the action on the field. He nods, "Will do." The batter swings hard, and the ball dribbles down the third baseline for a swinging bunt. Charlie applauds the hustle.

There is a pause in the conversation until Claude interjects, "She's leavin' town."

Charlie turns his attention from the field to his father. The puzzled look on his face tells Claude he has his son's full attention. "What?"

"I said she's leaving town."

"What'd you do?" Charlie questions accusingly.

"Nothing! We're fine. She just wants to travel more. See the world."

Charlie waves a hand. "Baloney! You musta done something." Claude holds his hands up in defense, eyes wide at the accusation. "Well, did she ask you to go along?"

Claude's expression softens, "Not exactly, but I wouldn't go anyway."

Charlie leans back as he absorbs the news. "Gee, Dad, that's too bad. I'm sorry to hear this. You guys seem to have a lot of fun together."

Charlie and Claude watch as Nat bats. They yell their cheers as he singles up the middle. The game wears on and finishes with Sisseton winning a shortened game, twelve to one. There is little conversation between the two men as they share some popcorn and the second game begins. Claude spots Susan and Veronica as they appear at the bottom of the grandstand. "Up here!" Claude hollers as he stands and waves. It's a little over done in the sparsely populated bleachers. The women point toward Claude and make their way up the stands.

The group settles in on the wooden bleachers after hugs and greetings are exchanged. "Nat pitched the first game. He got the win," Charlie informs the women.

"Ah," Veronica groans, "I'm sorry I missed it! Just trying to finish up this week's edition."

Charlie waves her comment away. "That's ok. He's playing centerfield this game."

"Did he get any hits?" Veronica queries.

"Three for five," Claude pipes in.

"Ooh, he had a good night! Would you two guys be interested in writing a story for the sports page?" Charlie and Claude laugh. "That's ok,

Susan will get the scorebook and put together a summary. We'll just stay a few minutes. We gotta a lot of work to do."

"What about supper?" Claude whines. "I'll buy at the casino."

Veronica flinches. "Wow! Did I hear you correctly? You said you'll buy?" Everyone laughs. "I'm sorry, Claude, we'll have to take a rain check." Veronica stands, "Come on, Susan, let's just head out now, since we missed Nat pitch anyway."

Susan joins Veronica. "Yeah, we better go."

Charlie and Claude get to their feet. Claude gives Susan a gentle nudge from his elbow and a nod toward Charlie. Susan is puzzled, but then she remembers, "Uh, Charlie, you working tomorrow?"

"Yeah."

"Mind if I stop by? I wanted to chat with you about...you know."

Charlie nods. "Sure. Anytime. I'll be around. They can radio me if I'm out, and I can be back at the station in just a few minutes."

Susan smiles. "I'll be there, say late morning?"

"Great." Charlie returns the smile. "See you tomorrow."

Kisses and goodbyes are exchanged. After the women leave, Charlie and Claude settle back in with their popcorn, and they resume watching the game. "Thanks," Claude remarks between mouthfuls.

"For what?" Charlie replies. "She's just going to talk to me."

"Thanks anyway." Claude smiles.

"You're welcome, Dad."

Chapter 49

Nine One One

Historic Downtown Sisseton, South Dakota

Susan climbs the stairs to her apartment. It has been a long night, working with Veronica trying to get the final edition ready for the printer. The four-block walk from the newspaper office in the cool summer night air was just what she needed to unwind from the stressful eighteen hour day. It was Veronica who said, "Good enough. Let's go home," that shut the day down.

That was at 1:30 in the morning. The files had been emailed, and the printer confirmed receipt. In twelve hours the paper copies would be transported to Sisseton, and ready for delivery. The day is over as Susan huffs and puffs a bit, dragging herself up the seventeen steps to her modest apartment above the hardware store. The ancient buildings of downtown Sisseton are remnants of a different era. Store owners worked on the street level and retired at night to accommodations above. Times changed as proprietors built separate houses to please family and diversify their income with rental properties. The historic downtown brick buildings are still effective income streams for the shrinking community.

This humble two room apartment is perfect for Susan. She can walk to work, and everything is covered, heat, water, trash, electricity. Everything is included in the rent at a very palatable price for a retired school teacher. Inside the apartment, she opens the window to let some fresh air come into the combined living room and kitchen area. After brushing her teeth, it is straight to bed in the only other room in the apartment, other than the bathroom. At 2:00 a.m., Susan notes the digital clock in the dark, but even on the verge of exhaustion, and with heavy eyelids, her body refuses to yield to sleep. Her mind reels with the thoughts of tomorrow's discussion with Charlie.

Variations of the future conversation bounce around her head for ten minutes. Imaginary conversations dramatically playing out in her brain abruptly end like an old record player scratching across the grooves on a vinyl record album. There is a noise in the living room. With an innate reaction, Susan reaches for her pistol in the nightstand drawer. Silently she closes the drawer and secures the weapon against her chest under the covers. She closes her eyes tightly and tries to remember if she shut and locked the door. She has become pretty casual in the small town, rarely locking her car door or her apartment. Maybe the door had just not latched and swung open in the breeze from the open window.

The streetlights below provide a constant glow even through her curtains. With her eyes wide open she stares at the bedroom door. She can see the door handle turn before she hears the creak of the ancient hinges. Susan is on her side curled up facing the door. Underneath the bed covers she grips her .45 caliber, semi automatic, Colt Model 1911, the former standard military-issue pistol. A hand holding a snub-nosed pistol pushes through the door, and she can see the weapon snag the light switch. With a flick of the gun's barrel the overhead bedroom light is on. Susan winces at the sudden change as her eyes adjust. The door flings open, and she can see the man holding the gun is Gabe Franzen. He is unsteady on his feet, pistol in one hand and a silver flask in the other. He brings the container to his lips. He chuckles; his eyes are crazy with what seems like a fire within as they dart around the room, but always returning to meet hers. He tips the flask and gulps down a large swallow. He grins, watching the woman in the bed squint at him. "Who is there? Who are you?" Susan questions, playing the part of a surprised woman. She recognizes the man and knows why he is there.

Gabe points the pistol at the woman. "I think you know, a monster from your worst nightmare."

"Please, don't hurt me. Just take whatever you want," Susan pleads. She exposes her left hand from the covers, as if surrendering. Her right hand steadies the pistol under the blankets. She is on her side and rests the pistol on her leg, lining it up the best she can, with the intruder in front of her.

Gabe shakes his head and tips the flask to his lips. "What I want is here in this room." The whiskey in the flask dribbles on his chin, and he wipes it with the sleeve of his black leather jacket. His eyes strain to focus, mind and body dulled by the alcohol. He laughs a snorting laugh. "At least Orloski came clean before he died. He told me." Gabe shouts, "You killed my uncle!" He spits the words figuratively and literally, spraying saliva from his mouth. He raises his shaking hand, pointing the pistol at the woman. "Now we are eve…"

Gabe can't get the words out. Bullets rip from beneath Susan's blankets as she squeezes the trigger over and over. Her aim from her hip is well placed. The slugs rip through Gabe's large body. His chest and abdomen suffer the direct and multiple shots. The wall behind him is sprayed with blood from the bullets tearing through his body. He is knocked backward against the dresser in the room and bouncing off the wall, he slumps to the floor. The blood splatter on the wall becomes a muddled mess as Gabe's body eases to the floor wiping the bloody spots with his bloody leather coat. He is dead before he hits the floor. The first shot found his heart. The seven other shots, four connecting with Gabe's body were superfluous. The final shot, as Gabe collapsed, tore a gaping hole in the left side of his skull. Brain matter and blood texture the bedroom wall.

Susan gasps for breath as the adrenaline is overwhelming. She is nauseous as her body's fight or flight instinct subsides, and her brain tries to reconcile the surreal situation. Her hands are shaking too much to hold the pistol, and it falls from her hand to the bed. She pushes herself out of the covers and reaches for her cell phone. Her hands are too shaky to press the buttons to dial 911. After four attempts, she finally succeeds and presses the send button.

On the other end of the line she hears a calm female voice, "Hello, this is 911, what is your emergency?"

"I just, I-I-I just shot," Susan stammers, "I just shot an intruder in my apartment. Please send help. I'm going to be sick."

Chapter 50

Aftermath

Charlie's Home

It is no more than ten minutes after Veronica crawls into bed next to a sleeping Charlie, that his cell phone buzzes on the night stand next to him. It's almost two o'clock in the morning, and Veronica is already asleep, oblivious to the phone's first vibration. The second signal from the phone stirs them both, and Charlie paws at the end table for his cell. "Phone," Veronica mumbles almost unintelligibly.

Charlie squints at the number in the caller ID a moment before answering, "Hello." Charlie listens. "I'm up now." He reaches for the light on the nightstand and moves to a sitting position on the edge of the bed, flicking the light on and illuminating the room. He rubs his face as he awakens. "I'll be right there."

Veronica snuggles deeper into the covers, relaxing, ready to fall back asleep. "You, get up," Charlie commands.

The words are far away in her ears. Veronica doesn't move a muscle. "You heard me." Charlie orders again, "Get up."

Veronica stirs, lifting her head ever so slightly. "Me?"

"It's your friend, Susan," Charlie emphasizes the name, and Veronica sits up.

"What happened?" she is fully alert now.

"She just shot somebody in her apartment. Get dressed. I'll get Claude up." Charlie pushes himself off the bed. He grabs at his uniform draped on a chair in the corner of the room. Veronica sits for a moment as the words sink in. She throws the covers off and scrambles to the bathroom.

*   *   *   *

At the corner of First Avenue and Oak Street in downtown Sisseton, emergency vehicles crowd the traveled way and sidewalks. Red and blue warning lights flash wildly, reflected off store front windows. Oak Street has been cordoned off completely with yellow police tape. The side entrance to the upstairs apartments is guarded by Roberts' County sheriff deputies.

Charlie pulls his BIA Police Tahoe up to the yellow ribbon as he approaches from the east on Oak Street, and a deputy hustles from his post at the entrance to lift the tape and allow Charlie to pull inside the crime scene area. Charlie flips the switch for his emergency lights to the off position, the clicking fades, and the cab indicator light disappears. He turns the engine off, and positions himself to address his passengers. He attempts to stifle a yawn, but the contagious action has everyone following Charlie's tired lead. Veronica sits in the front seat and Claude in the rear. He points a finger at them and gives his orders, addressing Veronica first. "I'll send for you in a bit. Five, ten minutes tops." Charlie turns to his father. "Dad, you'll only go up if she asks for you." Charlie eyes his passengers. "Got it?"

Charlie waits patiently until Veronica and Claude nod their acknowledgement. Charlie pulls the handle on his door, and opens it part way. He looks at his passengers. "I will send someone to get you. Do not come up until I send for you." It's one final wag of a finger at the passengers, and Charlie shuts the door and heads for the apartment entrance.

Chapter 51

The Scene

Relative to the chaos of the flashing lights of the emergency vehicles in the street, the walk up the stairs to the apartment for Charlie is serene. He enters the residence and immediately sees emergency personnel tending to Susan. All the lights in the small apartment are on, yet it still seems dark to Charlie. Susan seems diminutive. She is hunched over and covered by a blanket, breathing oxygen through a mask as an EMT takes her blood pressure. Her breaths are shallow, and Charlie can see the clear plastic oxygen mask fog and clear on each breath. He passes by Susan on her couch and looks in the bedroom where Jeremy stands over the face-down body of Gabe, a large pool of blood covers the laminate floor. There are footprints where the blood has been tracked through. Charlie points down at the bloody prints, but before he can say anything, Jeremy cuts him off, "Those are the tracks of the EMTs checking for a pulse." Jeremy shrugs, "Nothing we can do about it." He smiles at Charlie and gives him a nod. "Hey, Boss. I didn't imagine seeing you again tonight."

Charlie stares down at the body in the cramped bedroom. Without looking up he grunts, "Gabe Franzen."

"In the flesh...and blood," Jeremy chuckles at his joke.

"She say anything?" Charlie continues to stare at the body at his feet.

"Nada."

"Gun?" Charlie questions, finally looking up at Jeremy.

Jeremy is holding two clear plastic evidence bags, one in each hand. He lifts one higher. "Tagged and bagged. Susan had a .45 caliber Colt model 1911. The kind the military used." Charlie nods knowingly. Jeremy hoists the other bag up, letting the other drop to his side. "Tagged this guy's also," Jeremy gives a nod to the body on the floor. Berretta nine millimeter." Jeremy shakes his head and frowns. "Clear case of self defense...in my humble opinion."

Charlie's eyes scan the room. He sees the blood splattered wall and the bullet holes for the first time, "Yeah, we'll see." His eyes move to the bed, and he can see the tattered bed spread. He holds up a finger. "I don't want anybody else up here. Once the EMTs are gone, you stay here and guard the apartment. We'll let the FBI and DCI handle it. Good job securing the weapons, Jeremy. Hold on to them and make sure you get a receipt when you turn them over to Agent Brown." Charlie smiles at Jeremy.

"Will do, Boss." Jeremy smiles, accepting the compliment.

Charlie turns and moves to the couch where Susan sits. He takes a knee next to her, close to the young EMT still monitoring her blood pressure. He reaches for her hand and holds it in his right hand and uses his left hand to gently pat hers. Her hand is shaking, and Charlie notices her whole body seems to be shivering. "You all right?" Susan nods. Charlie forces a weak smile. "I told you I'd see you tomorrow, and I guess it is technically tomorrow."

Susan pulls the oxygen mask away, the corners of her mouth turn upward in the slightest smile. "He just came in the apartment. I don't even know if I locked the door. I guess I may have been lax about it." She shakes her head in disbelief. "I was exhausted from working late on the paper with Veronica." Susan places the mask back over her face and breathes several times before continuing. "The floors and doors are squeaky, so I heard something and got my gun from the nightstand. He was drunk and not too stealthy." She returns the oxygen mask over her nose and mouth.

"Why didn't you call 911?" Charlie asks.

Susan shakes her head and pulls the mask away, "I grabbed my gun...I," she pauses and points to something she imagines as her eyes move from Charlie's to the doorway of the bedroom. "I think my phone was up there, on the dresser."

Charlie looks toward the bedroom and sees the dresser. He turns back to Susan, "He must not have given much thought to you having a gun." Charlie continues to pat her hand.

Susan smiles again. "Not many would give a second thought to an old lady having a gun...and he was drunk." She frowns and shakes her head, "He pushed open the bedroom door and flicked on the light with his pistol. He had a silver flask that he drank from before he pointed the pistol at me. Did you find it?"

"The gun?" Charlie questions.

"No, the flask."

Charlie shakes his head, "We got his pistol. I suppose the flask bounced under the bed. We're gonna leave everything. We'll let the FBI take care of it. What can you tell me about your gun?" Charlie asks as politely as he can.

"It was my uncle's." Susan frowns again. "He's dead. He was in the army. Korea."

Charlie nods. He glances at the EMTs still monitoring Susan. "Listen, I got Veronica downstairs along with Claude. You want them to come up."

Susan shakes her head and puts the oxygen mask back in place. "Are you going to the hospital?" Charlie looks back and forth between the EMTs, who shrug. Susan shakes her head again. "I'll tell you what. If you are not going to the hospital, maybe you should spend the night at Veronica's. I'll send her up."

Charlie stares at Susan, waiting for a response. Finally she nods and Charlie stands. "I'll send her up."

*　　*　　*　　*

On the street, back at his Tahoe, Charlie opens the front passenger's door and is met with two pairs of questioning eyes. "She's going to be fine...I think." Charlie thrusts his chin toward Veronica. "Veronica, Susan wants you upstairs." Veronica unfastens her seat belt and scrambles to exit the vehicle, but is impeded by Charlie. "She's going to stay with you." Charlie points an admonishing finger at Veronica. "Tell her I heard about her plans to leave town, but you tell her she can't leave yet."

Veronica flinches at the words. She didn't know Susan was planning to leave town and her face scrunches. "Leave town?"

"Just tell her," Charlie orders sternly. "I'm sure you guys will have a nice long chat." Charlie moves out of the way, and Veronica bounds away toward the apartment entrance. "Sorry, Dad. She was pretty shaken up. I'll take you home and drop you off."

Claude nods, acknowledging the situation with a frown.

Chapter 52

The Interview

BIA Police Station – Sisseton, South Dakota

Behind the closed door of Skip's vacant office, Charlie sits, slumped in his boss's chair. Across the desk in the visitor's chair, FBI Agent Brown slouches as well. The two figures of bad posture sit in silence. The men are practically mirror images of each other, hands folded resting on their respective bellies. Agent Brown breaks the silence, his hands gesticulate wildly. "I just can't believe this. What the hell is going on out here?" He straightens in his chair. Sitting on the chairs edge, he leans on the desk.

Charlie is unphased by the outburst. He just shakes his head and speaks slowly in an almost hypnotic tone, "I find myself asking that same question nearly every day."

Agent Brown looks at his watch. "So, is she coming in?" He shakes down the sleeve of his suit jacket back over the timepiece on his wrist.

"Fancy watch ya got there. Is it a Rolex?"

"It is. It was a gift from my wife."

"Nice," Charlie responds, still in a depressed demeanor. He holds up his wrist, exposing his watch. "Ten dollar Timex. I bought it for myself."

"Super." Agent Brown frowns. "Is she coming in or not?"

"She called and told me she'd talk at ten o'clock this morning."

Brown looks at his watch again. "Getting close." He slumps back in his chair. "Skip still out?"

"Yup."

"How is Betty?"

"Not good." Charlie's mouth twists down.

"She got a lawyer?" Brown asks.

"Skip's wife?" Charlie winces. "Why would she need a lawyer? For her will?"

"No," Brown whines in annoyance. "Your girl. The shooting-nun. Does she have a lawyer?"

Charlie shrugs, "Don't know."

Agent Brown fidgets in his chair, resettling into a lean on the desk again. "I got a piece of news for you." Charlie's eyebrows go up. "The technicians combed that drainage like we talked about. They found both slugs."

"Really?" Charlie's voice goes higher.

"Yup," Brown smiles. "The slugs were beaten up pretty good. Flatter than pancakes, but there was enough to match them to Gabe's Berretta."

Charlie's folded hands form a steeple with his fingers, collapsing and reforming the pointed configurations. Charlie stares at his hands. "I can't imagine that news sitting well with Carl Franzen."

Agent Brown shakes his head. "What are you talking about? I don't think Franzen's gonna give a flying flip about Orloski. His son is dead."

Charlie looks at the agent, sitting across the desk from him. "You wanna tell Susan she's going to have a price on her head, or do I get to do that?" Charlie stares at the agent, and Brown stares back. There is silence for a minute, "You're sitting in on the interview, right?"

Brown exhales and nods. "Yeah, I'll be in the room with you."

*   *   *   *

Interview Room One is full with only three people. The tiny, gray, antiseptic room is adorned with a table and two chairs. Agent Brown stands in the corner, leaning against the mirrored glass opposite the observation area. Susan sits at the table facing the mirror. Charlie sits across from Susan. He opens the conversation. "I don't know if you know Agent Brown. He's with the FBI." Charlie gestures behind him to Brown in his dark suit. The FBI agent attempts to look as casual as possible, leaning against the wall, most weight on one foot, one leg crossed in front of the other. Susan thinks to herself that this man, with his arms folded and nonchalant pose, couldn't be a more stereotypical FBI agent. Brown nods toward Susan upon Charlie's introduction.

Susan nods back, meeting Brown's eyes and then looking to Charlie. "Yes, he introduced himself earlier."

"You had told me you wanted to speak to me previously." Charlie fidgets in the hard metal chair, not knowing how to start the dialogue. "Now with the events of last night, we can expand our conversation, if that's ok with you?" Susan nods. "Have you talked to a lawyer?"

"Do I need a lawyer?" Susan asks unflinchingly. "I'm not under arrest am I?"

"No, no." Charlie holds up his hands. "This is just a casual conversation." Charlie glances over his shoulder at Brown and back to Susan. "This conversation is off the record." Charlie looks over his shoulder at Brown again. The FBI agent gives a slow nod to Charlie. "We're not recording this; nobody is on the other side of the glass watching. It's just us trying to clear things up. Put all this to bed."

"Very well, then." Susan looks back and forth between her interrogators. She is calm. Her demeanor is matter-of-fact, straight to the point. "What do you want to know?" She punctuates her question with a shrug.

"We are not here to talk about self defense in your apartment," Charlie's voice is soft and slow, "but, we have questions about the other Franzen." Charlie glances back toward Agent Brown, who meets Charlie's eyes for a moment and nods before returning his gaze to Susan. His expressionless face is unreadable, and Susan glares at the agent a moment before turning her attention and smile back to Charlie. Charlie continues, "We got your .45. The brass we found at Father Franzen's cabin had similar extraction markings to the casings we recovered in your apartment."

Susan's smile widens. "Do you have a question for me?" She folds her arms. "I don't know anything about a priest being shot. In fact, I heard Father Franzen died of a heart attack." Susan leans forward in her chair, she folds her hands and places them on the table. "I don't know what you want me to say or what you want from me. I have asked and been forgiven by God for any and all of my transgressions. I am at peace."

Agent Brown is staring at Susan indirectly now. He uses the mirror to observe her, arms still folded, still leaning against the wall. He speaks toward the reflection in the mirror, "I'm afraid the law may not be as forgiving as the man upstairs." Brown pauses, turns, and makes direct eye contact with Susan. "However, in this case, the reason I'm in this room is to tell you that the U.S. Attorney has no interest in pursuing a case against a former nun that shot a known gangster in self defense and may or may not have contributed to an expedited death of a child molester." Brown pulls a notebook from his inside jacket pocket and flips it open to a page. "In fact let me quote what the U.S. Attorney told me." Agent Brown glances at Susan. "And I quote," he begins as he reads from his notebook, "I'll be God damned if I try to prosecute a nun puttin' down a pedophile and a murdering gangster."

Susan nods and smiles. "You have a question for me, Agent Brown?"

Agent Brown stashes his notebook back in his jacket pocket, his blank expression thaws into a hint of smile, as he enjoys the verbal sparring from this woman. "Yes," Brown's hands drop to his sides and he digs them into his pockets. "What was your relationship with Father Franzen? There is a letter in evidence that said you were coming to see him to, and I quote, 'make things right.' Is there something you want to tell us?"

Susan shrugs. "It's no secret that I was a nun and he was a priest, and many years ago we worked together. I did go see him...by his invitation." Susan emphasizes the words. She pauses, pursing her lips. "That's about it."

Brown pulls one hand from his pocket and holds it up questioning. "What were you going to make right?"

"Confession." Susan folds her arms and frowns. "I needed to make my confession. I knew what he had done all those years ago, and I wanted him to hear my confession. I had done nothing to stop him." The first hint of anger starts to appear in Susan's voice. "In case you are not familiar, Agent Brown, confession is a big part of the Catholic religion." Agent Brown opens his mouth to ask a follow up question, but Susan holds up a hand to silence him. "Then, he confessed to me. What can I say? The weight of the world seemed to come off his shoulders, and the Lord took him."

Charlie speaks before he can even think, "You were there?" The words are thick, his voice husky.

"Yes."

Agent Brown sports a confused look. "Why didn't you call an ambulance?"

Susan meets the FBI agents eyes, and there is a moment they stare at each other before she responds, "He couldn't be saved."

Charlie and Agent Brown look at each other. The room is silent as Susan looks back and forth between each man. "Is that all? Am I free to go?"

Silence weighs heavy on the room. Susan pushes her chair back from the table, and she readies to push herself up. Charlie glances to Brown, who nods. Charlie turns back to Susan and nods, but before Susan can stand Agent Brown interjects, "Susan."

Susan halts her effort in gathering momentum to stand and meets the man's eyes. "Do you realize you killed the son of a crime boss?"

"I do."

Agent Brown's head shakes as he talks. "The killing, justified or not in the eyes of the law, is going to have ramifications. Do you understand what I'm saying?"

"I do."

The FBI agent stares down at the woman. Brown is puzzled by the woman's relative obliviousness to the gravity of the situation. He looks away, scratches the back of his neck, and tries to emphasize the point again. "I want you to imagine the Franzen family looking to avenge a favorite son's death and add that to the fact that you are linked to the death of that son's uncle."

"Agent Brown," Susan smiles, "I'm not a child; I understand what you are saying. I'll have a price on my head, but you seem to forget something."

Agent Brown flinches, and he asks the question, "What is that?"

Susan stands and smiles, beaming, "I have God on my side." She looks back and forth between Charlie and the agent. "Is there anything else?"

Agent Brown looks to Charlie. "Charlie?"

Charlie stands. "You're free to go." He opens the door, and Susan gives a last glance over her shoulder and a wave to the two men standing in stunned silence in the room.

Chapter 53

Shorthanded

Sisseton, South Dakota – One Month Later

Charlie sits in the Roberts County Standard Newspaper office. His chair swivels back and forth impatiently. Across the desk from him sits Veronica typing on her computer. She stares at the screen as her fingers dance across the keyboard. "It's been fifteen minutes," Charlie whines. "Are we going to get coffee or what?"

Veronica doesn't look up from the computer, but shakes her head. "I'm sorry. As you can see, I'm a little shorthanded. All by myself now."

The office radio provides the melody of Tracy Lawrence and his song "Sticks and Stones." The country music softly permeates the office and fades into the more harsh classic country sounds of Gary Stewart and his song "She's Acting Single." Charlie dials back his whininess, "I know." He stops swiveling back and forth. "Do you know where she went?"

Charlie dials back his whininess, "I know." He stops swiveling back and forth. "Do you know where she went?"

Veronica still doesn't look up. "She refused to say...at least she didn't tell me. For everyone's protection; that's what she said."

"She told me," Charlie smiles smugly. He begins to swivel in his chair again.

Charlie's comment gets Veronica's attention. She stops typing and looks at him. "Are you serious?"

Charlie rotates in his chair. "She told me something. I don't know if it's true."

"What'd she say?" Charlie just smiles and spins in his chair. "Charlie, c'mon. Tell me."

Charlie shrugs. "She just said she was going to hide in plain sight." Veronica flinches. "What is that supposed to mean?"

"She's gonna live her life. She mentioned the Southwest...Phoenix area is what she hinted at." Charlie stops his chair from spinning, planting his feet firmly on the floor. He waves his hand in frustrated objection. "Enough about that! You going to hire somebody soon? It's starting to cut into our quality time!"

Charlie's tantrum catches Veronica by surprise as she stares blankly at him a moment, but a smile quickly brightens her face. "You're right. Let's go." She stands and steps around the desk, extending her hand to Charlie.

Charlie reaches for her hand. "I don't know why you can't just take a break. For crying out loud, you did a story for CNN...maybe you can rest on your laurels a bit."

Veronica pulls Charlie to his feet. "The news stops for no man...or woman. I'm gonna get somebody hired, don't worry. Maybe a couple of part-timers."

"Yay!" Charlie emits a mock cheer. "Maybe we can actually take a vacation together!"

Veronica wraps her arm around Charlie's waist. "Now about this coffee you are buying me..." She pulls him toward the exit.

Charlie moves in stride with her. "Wait, I said nothing about me buying coffee. I assumed you'd pay."

Veronica rolls her eyes as they go out the door.

Chapter 54

Lakeside Sunset

The day is done and Charlie is back home at his trailer. Entering his home he is greeted to the blaring television as Nat and Claude sit in a chair and on the couch respectively, staring at a rerun of the cartoon *Family Guy*. Charlie shakes his head in disgust as his father and nephew can't even turn away from the TV for a second to acknowledge his presence. "I'm home!" he shouts. Charlie scowls at the couch potatoes.

Claude turns and gives a wave at Charlie. "Hey, Charlie. Have you seen this cartoon with the baby and talking dog? It's hilarious!"

Charlie's hands go to his hips. "Get your fishing stuff! I heard they're bitin' up at Cottonwood. Big perch. Come on you lumps; get off your butts!"

Claude and Nat finally stir, but not fast enough for Charlie. He moves over to the couch, grabs the remote, and shuts off the TV.

*   *   *   *

The sun begins to set. Charlie is up along the shore running a hook through a minnow. He casts his line and nods acknowledging his precision aim. The bobber settles in on the smooth lake. He places the fishing rod in the holder next to his father's. Moving back to a folding lawn chair nestled on a short stretch of sandy beach, he joins his dad sitting side by side a few steps from their rods. A few yards away, they watch Nat cast a jig tipped with a minnow along a stand of cattails. "Ahhh," Charlie sighs. "Now this is the life. Family, fishing, and a couple of big perch on the stringer. Does it get any better than this?" He slaps a hand down on his dad's knee and squeezes it. Charlie points to Claude's bobber twitching on the water. "Hey, Dad, I think you got a bite."

Greg Heitmann has worked for the Federal Government for 20 plus years, which pays the bills while pursuing a career in writing. His life experiences have been an inspiration for much of his writing. Look for something new from Greg soon!

Made in the USA
Charleston, SC
14 December 2016